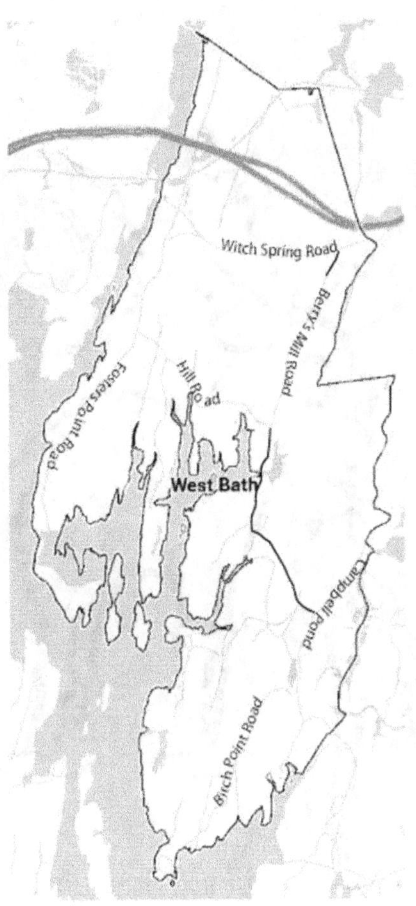
Witch Spring Road
Berry's Mill Road
Fosters Point Road
Hill Road
West Bath
Campbell Pond
Bich Point Road

My kid drew this!

artwork by Chanda Hinton

Zombie Moose

Of
West Bath, Maine

ISBN 978-0-9882036-2-4
Published by
Marsha Hinton
DBA New Meadows Media
PO Box 535
Lewiston, ME 04243-0535
United States of America

writer@marshahinton.com

Chapter 1

"Quinn, have you called Mrs. Menard yet? I'm almost there, and I don't want to surprise her."

"Just called the mad, old cow. She's expecting you," Quinn Crawford said.

Gaige LaRoche maneuvered the oil delivery truck down the narrow road to Mrs. Menard's place. Despite the heat of the day, Gaige rolled up the truck windows. His glance flicked from the yard to the truck's rearview mirror before backing into his customer's driveway.

Mrs. Menard was in her eighties, and to protect herself from robbers and murderers, she employed a long stick. If you surprised her, she would lean out the window and pound on the nearby [1]bee hives with the stick, sending the bees into an angry frenzy. It took Gaige only once to learn that he needed to make certain she knew he was coming.

Gaige sweltered in the hot truck, his eyes locked

------

1   **Bees**: They want to make honey and baby bees. Have an averion to crazy old women beating on hives.

on Mrs. Menard's front door as it barely opened. Mrs. Menard's vicious Teacup Chihuahua shot out the door like a lightning bolt to attack his truck. Gaige looked down at the growling dog, whose lips were pulled back from its razor sharp teeth. Over and over again, the little beast hurled itself at the vehicle, it's beady black eyes fixed on Gaige, who rolled down the window and waved at Mrs. Menard as she approached to retreive her pet.

Over the barking of the tiny dog, Gaige shouted, "Is that a new collar for Mr. Biggies? Sure is [2]cunnin.'" Mrs. Menard beamed. She called to the attack dog, picking him up before Gaige exited the truck.

Mrs. Menard peered at Gaige through thick glasses. "You're that boy who did the protest over those clam flats in North Bath," she said. "You ain't here to protest, are you?"

Gaige managed a smile. "I'm here to fill up your fuel oil tank," he shouted.

"Oh, yes, that nice boy called and said you were coming," Mrs. Menard said.

Gaige handed Mrs. Menard a dog biscuit as Mr. Biggies quivered and snapped. "Oh Mr. Biggies, you're right lively today." Gaige smiled at Mrs. Menard, "That is one [3]wicked adorable dog," he said. Still beaming,

---

2   **Cunnin:** Maine lingo for cuteness.

3   **Wicked**: Regional substitute for "very."

Mrs. Menard and the snarling Mr. Biggies went back inside.

Gaige returned to the truck to call the dispatcher. "Quinn, just got the okay. By the way, Mrs. Menard thinks you're a boy."

"Nice. Thanks for the shot to my ego," Quinn laughed then making her voice as deep as she could said, "Give me a call when you're done."

Exiting the vehicle, Gaige slipped on a longsleeved white shirt and placed a mosquito net over his head before resettling his hat. Careful not to make any sudden moves, Gaige made his way gingerly around the bee hives to the fill spout for the oil tank. He looked toward the kitchen window where Mrs. Menard stood, sending a smile her way in reassurance. Sweat running down his back, he could feel the prickle of thousands of little bee eyes watching him, waiting for him to make them angry as the oil trickled into the basement tank.

Mrs. Menard continued to peer out the kitchen window at Gaige, who occasionally looked her way and kept smiling to remind her he wasn't there to murder her. After what seemed to be years, he finished the fill and carefully treaded his way around the hives to the truck.

Mrs. Menard was waiting on the porch with a plate of cookies while Mr. Biggies remained inside yipping and clawing at the closed door. Mr. Biggies was able to multitask and while he was attacking the door, he was also plotting the murder of Mrs. Menard. He just wanted to practice by murdering Gaige first.

"Here boy, have some cookies," Mrs. Menard said, thrusting a paper plate at him.

Gaige surveyed the cookies arranged on a Christmas doily under plastic wrap. "Did you bake these just for me, Mrs. Menard?" Gaige said as he warily eyed the stale looking cookies.

Mrs. Menard's eyes shifted away from him. "Someone gave these to me and there are too many for me to eat."

"Ah. Well, thank you, Mrs. Menard." Gaige took the plate.

"Go ahead and have one. They're good."

Glancing at the bee hives, Gaige rolled up the mosquito net covering his head. Forcing a grin, he peeled back the plastic wrap and took one. Mrs. Menard beamed at him as he took his first bite and nearly broke a tooth.

"I always like a crispy cookie, don't you?" she said.

Gaige nodded as he tried to swallow the jaw-breaker of a cookie, wondering if the sharp edges were lacerating his throat. Mrs. Menard eyed him, and satisfied he had downed the petrified treat, she returned to the house, closing the door firmly behind her. Gaige set the plate of ancient cookies on the truck seat then lowered the netting back over his face before returning to finish winding the hose into the truck.

Sliding behind the steering wheel, he picked up the mic. "Quinn, I'm going to stop by my apartment before the next run."

"Still looking for that job offer, huh?"

"No. It's lunch time. I'm just around the corner. I thought I'd run by and grab a bite."

Gaige could just about hear the twinkle in Quinn's eyes.

"Uh huh. I bet you have enough rejections to paper your kitchen by now. Why don't you apply to that pet food company if you're so bent on getting a scientific type job? Didn't the company recruiter say that they would be interested in talking with you after you graduated? I heard they pay pretty well."

Gaige slumped in the seat, letting his head thump against the steering wheel. Gaige had a degree in animal biology with a focus on evolutionary biology and ecology. It wasn't the economy that had prevented him from getting work befitting his degree. In high school, Gaige had gained infamy in the scientific community when he had led a failed effort to prevent a residential development from being built near a clam flat. It was a huge media event that wrongfully painted Gaige as an environmental kook and publicity hog.

"Thanks for the encouragement," he moaned.

"No problem," said Quinn. "By the way, did Mrs. Menard give you any treats?"

"A plate of holiday cookies. I hope they're only from last Christmas," he groaned.

Quinn laughed. "Made you eat one, did she?

Chapter 2

[4]Dave Levesque, carefully wiped his hands before grabbing the teapot. Just a trickle of tea dribbled into his cup. Dave lifted the lid and peered into the depths of the old brown pot then sighed. Replacing the lid, he said, "Ms. Day, since the veritable staffing situation is in a state of stasis, may I extend a value proposition?"

Lottie Day gave Dave a puzzled look.

"I propose that I refill the undertooled teapot so that we may avoid any personal inertia that inhibits productization and foster sustainablity toward the bottom line."

Lottie's fingers, covered with icing, attempted to remove the lid of the teapot. Her greasy, sugary fingers left a slick film.

Giving up after a few tries she said, "You saying

4   Dave was a good student in school, but never really distinguished himself in any particular discipline. He discovered the delights of the Thesaurus and became a real genius at verbal obfuscation.

you'll make more tea?"

Dave nodded.

"I could stand another cup," she said.

Dave stood and used the moist towel lying on the table to wipe the white residue off the teapot.

Lottie's eyes went to the old brown teapot then darted to the kettle on the stove. Nodding, she pointed a sticky finger at the tea on the shelf and went back to spreading the filling on the maple [5]whoopie pies again. She looked up as she heard the front door open.

"Ma? Ma, where are you?" "In the kitchen, Son."

Larry Day continued down the hall toward the kitchen and stopped at the entry. His eyes rested suspiciously on the man standing at the stove. "Who's this?"

Lottie's puzzled expression changed into a toothy grin. "Oh, you know your Aunt Nelda usually comes down to help make whoopie pies every year."

"Ayuh." Larry frowned and pointed at Dave. "That ain't Aunt Nelda."

"Well, Son, Sissy is about to have that baby any day now and since Nelda couldn't be here on account of her being so far away, she sent Dave."

Smiling, Dave turned and extended his hand to the young man.

---

5   **Whoopie Pie Desert Sandwich**: Usually chocolate cake, with a super sweet filling of shortening based icing. Lazy bakers use whipped cream.

"Hello. I'm Dave Levesque, [6]P.F.M.S."

Ignoring him, Larry said, "Uh huh. Looks like a televangelist in a frilly apron."

The smile evaporated as Dave's right eyebrow inched toward his hairline. Shrugging, he withdrew his hand and turned back to the tea kettle.

"Stop staring, Larry. It's rude. And I'll have you know that's your aunt's best apron. Dave has been a big help. Here, have a whoopie pie."

The young man continued to bore holes in Dave's back with his eyes. "Ma, you know I don't like those awful things. Where are the chocolate ones?"

"In the icebox. The tourists like the maple ones and Memorial Day is almost here. I heard that Walter is already selling them over on Fosters Point. Which reminds me; can you get my road signs out of the barn and repaint them today?"

Larry turned to the window. "Today! Ma, it's raining out there. Paint won't dry."

The old woman's eyes looked out the window to the leaden sky. "Is not. It's just a bit of sea smoke. The deck isn't wet. The paint will dry."

The young man rolled his eyes. "I'm headin' to town first. I'll get to them this afternoon," he said opening the refrigerator.

"What's that smell?" Larry cautiously moved

____

6   **P.F.M.S**: Professional Freelance Meeting Substitute. Dave made this up so he would have something cool after his name.

containers around in the crowded refrigerator until he found an oozing plastic tub in the back. He picked up a pair of tongs from the counter and carefully removed the bulging vessel of leftovers from the fridge.

"Ma, please tell me this isn't sourdough starter."

"Oh, my. That's [7]boiled dinner. It was so good I didn't want to throw it out."

"Boiled dinner from when?" Larry considered the offensive container.

"Oh, let's see. Um, last November if I remember correctly."

"Ma, it's May! This mess looks like it's alive."

Dave's attention moved from watching the tea kettle to the disgusting ingredients in the tub.

"It might still be good. It will make a fine supper," Lottie explained.

Larry thrust the container towards his mother. "A junkyard dog wouldn't eat this. You should have thrown this mess out months ago."

Dave's eyes were watering as he made gagging noises. Holding his nose, he moved slowly away from Larry and the tub he was waving around.

"I'm throwing this out." He used a fork to lift the lid slightly, and a thin puff of yellowish-gray vapor swirled around the opening. "This has gone off."

---

7   Boiled dinner: Regional fall/winter comfort food consisting of boiled cabbage, onions, various root vegetables and ham or beef.

Dave increased his speed. He knocked over a chair as he fled from Larry.

"Ms. Day, my contractual agreement with your dear sibling didn't foresee being in the proximity of toxic materials. You will have to finalize the whoopie pies by yourself. I will be taking my leave now. You are on your own. Your sister will get a prorated bill."

Dave covered his mouth with his hand, mumbling unintelligently as he exited through the back door.

"Toxic waste! Well! I like that! That's my boiled dinner. Everyone likes my boiled dinner!" Lottie shouted.

"Ma, he can't hear you. The televangelist is out to his car by now. And it WAS your boiled dinner." Larry eyed the container again. "I don't have any idea what it is now."

"Hold up there. Don't pour that down the sink. It'll ruin the septic. Go pitch it out back in the woods," she said pulling a dish towel over her nose. "And put the lid back on it."

Larry hurried across the mowed lawn and walked several feet into the tree line until the brambles stopped him. He took aim for the woods and whipped the putrid mess as far as he could.

He looked at the gray goo dripping from the tongs and threw them after the container.

Spiraling through the woods, the tub landed safely in the tangle of limbs in an old willow tree. The spinning tongs struck the container seconds later. The lid exploded off the tub, freeing the viscous contents.

The fresh green leaves of the willow were now coated with the slimy boiled dinner. Drying rapidly, it seemed to actually sizzle. The sounds of buzzing insects ceased. They died right and left as they attempted to escape from the fumes.

Chapter 3

Deep in the woods, a gray cloud of insects swarmed around a young bull moose. Raw patches were beginning to grow on the moose's hide as the [8]black flies' stabbing, venom-filled bites continued to multiply. Rings of the pests chewed at large red wounds, bringing fresh blood to the surface.

Driven by pain, the moose made his way toward the edge of the woods without his usual caution.

His attempts to rub against trees and brambles proved ineffective against the flying carnivores. No amount of swishing his tail, twitching his ears or rippling his hide was able to displace the bugs. He snorted almost continuously to try to rid them from his nose. Unable to remain still, he continued forward even though the trees were beginning to thin.

8	**Black Fly**: Insect family of Simuliidae.; 40 species in Maine appear during the latter days of mud season. Painful bite. Not to be confused with Sho-Fly-Pie and never with Spanish fly.

Zombie Moose

The large creature seemed to shimmer as the flies moved around his torso and massive head. The moose sensed he needed to find a pond deep enough to immerse himself to be free of the torment of relentless stinging that was driving him to madness.

When he caught the scent of a willow, the moose reckoned there would be water nearby. He turned slightly and headed toward the smell, but as he came closer, he could tell the scent of the willow was wrong. He paused to consider, but the persistent biting of the flies drove him forward.

The sight of the cleared yard brought his head up quickly. The flies were only momentarily thwarted by the sharp movement, and rapidly settled back to their feasting. The moose had learned to be wary. Turning from the open area, he thrust his head around to find the scent of the willow.

There it was, slightly off to the right just out of sight of the house. His hide was in constant motion in an attempt to dislodge the flies as he made his way to the tree.

The moose scanned the area around the willow for a pond, still noting the different smell. Blinking the flies from his eyes, he moved forward, sniffing at the small stream trickling beside the willow. He lifted his head to continue scanning for a pond and realized that the flies were gone.

He cast his massive head around, and considered the area. It was very close to the tree line. He knew he would be safer in the dark of the woods. He turned and moved back towards the forest when the flies descended on him. Leaping away on spindly legs, the moose retreated to the willow.

He regarded the area around the willow. Enough of the fly venom was coursing through his veins that he knew he needed to rest. There was cover here, a stream of water, and he had always liked willow leaves. The absence of black flies made up for the reduced security of the thick woods. He lapped at the stream and lifted his head to sniff the willow.

The tree had a strange taste. The moose snorted and moved to a new limb. He pulled another sample into his mouth and grunted. After a moment, he began to methodically strip the leaves from the drooping limbs.

Sleepy from the fly venom and the meal of willow leaves, the moose explored the limits of the no-fly zone. He identified a comfortable resting place near the protection of the willow tree. Settling into the soft grass and moss near the stream, and full from the leaves, he was finally able to rest.

The dreams of the moose weren't as pleasant as his surroundings. Feverish images filled his mind. His hide rippled in pace with the visions that assailed his subconscious. Spasmodic twitching of his legs increased in severity until his entire body convulsed.

His stomach roiled. The sharp pains in his gut bringing the moose to a state of semi-consciousness before he vomited. Still in a stupor, the moose struggled to his feet and stumbled aimlessly outside the safety of the willow tree. The black flies swarmed when the one-ton creature moved toward them. Most of them fled at the wrongness of his scent, those that bit the moose died.

A vague sense of hunger coursed through the moose's brain. It needed to feed. The moose turned back to the willow. The vegetation wasn't what he wanted. The moose looked around, rejecting nearby food sources. Moving in an intoxicated daze, the moose turned away from the willow, looking for something to sate its hunger.

The moose continued to move in jerky motions toward the tree line and the cleared lawn he had seen earlier. No longer cautious, he knew food would be in that direction.

"Well, I'll be!" Lottie Day said. From the kitchen window, she watched the moose stagger from the woods and collapse at the edge of her dooryard. She ran out onto the deck and watched the moose lying motionless.

Lottie yelled. "Moose, are you dead?" The moose didn't move.

"Can't have a dead moose in my dooryard," she declared to the unhearing moose. She walked back inside and punched numbers into the phone.

"Town of West Bath, Town Clerk speaking," Mark Hanigan said.

"Mark, this is Lottie Day over at Birch Point. I've got a dead moose in my dooryard. Can you get hold of animal control?"

"What? A dead moose? I'll call Gaige or Scott and get one of them out there. Don't know what they can do; may need them both. A [9]moose is kind of large. I'll just call both of them," Mark said. "I think I'll get the sheriff to go out as well."

Lottie looked out her window at the motionless moose near the tree line. "Well, I can't move the thing," she muttered.

---

9   **Maine Moose**: Boy howdy, is it large. An adult bull moose weighs in easily at over a ton. Reclusive and shy. Only real danger posed is during rutting season, when there are calves present, or when they come in contact with a moving vehicle.

Chapter 4

Keith Neves came out from the [10]Selectman's office as soon as Mark hung up the phone. "Did I just hear you talking about a dead moose here in West Bath?"

"Indeed you did. Haven't had one of those yet. First time for everything," Mark smiled as he started to punch the number for the animal control officers into the phone.

"Hold on a minute, Mark. Let's make sure none of those environmental guys get involved. Last thing we need is another newsworthy scandal like that stupid clam flat thing. Good thing Gaige got caught tampering with the clams or I would have lost my shirt on that

---

10   **Selectmen**: Many towns in New England have a town meeting/selectboard type of government wherein all the citizens are the legislative body and the selectmen make the wishes of the citizens happen. Sometimes, as in the case of Keith, the selectmen get a little big for their britches.

project." Keith rubbed his chin. "Let's take a moment to plan how we'll handle the media. We need to keep this managed," Keith said.

Mark licked his bottom lip. He thought about reminding Keith that Gaige had not tampered with anything, but decided to focus on the more important issue.

"Mr. Neves, it's a dead moose. The neighbors will notice," Mark said.

"We need to protect West Bath from negative fodder for the papers. This has the potential of blowing right up," Keith said.

"It will smell," Mark said.

"Exactly!" Keith said.

"No, I mean the moose," Mark said.

Keith rolled his eyes.

"I'm not saying leave it there. We just need to be discreet. Do you think you could let Scott and Gaige know they need to keep a lid on this? Don't discuss this with anyone, you know, for the sake of the town?" Keith said.

Mark paused to consider what his response should be when the town office door opened and Harriet McElroy walked in. Keith's eyes went wide as he backed away from the clerk's counter. "Good. Is Frank in his office?" Keith asked. Mark nodded. "The man has been here all day. He knows Frank is here," thought Mark. Keith turned and hustled toward the [11]town

---

11   **Town Administrator**: Hired by selectmen to do what

administrator's office.

"Dude, it's a dead moose, not WikiLeaks," thought Mark. Smiling, he turned to Harriet.

Long ago, Harriet's lineage had kept intersecting with an exceptionally dower clan of Scots and a group of really cranky Puritans. When this intersecting gene pool reached Harriet, the DNA combined to bless Harriet with a remarkably severe expression and authoritative voice even when she was a small child. As she aged, she developed a tick in her jaw and a squinty left eye. This made her unyielding visage even more terrifying. Behind her back, those who feared her assigned the unkind nickname of, "Stink Eye Harriet."

Selectman Keith feared her. Not that she had ever done anything to Keith. She actually wished him no harm. Regardless of her goodwill toward him, he believed she could see all the way to the dark corners of his soul. He just knew that Harriet was waiting for the right time when she would reveal his secrets to the world.

Despite Keith's opinion and her frightening appearance, Harriet was the very definition of kindness, goodness, and charity. People who knew her well would tell you that you would be hard pressed to find someone sweeter or more giving than Harriet.

Mark did not fear Harriet.

---

they were elected to do. Selectmen can then spend their time managing photo ops.

"Good morning, Ms. McElroy. How can I help you today?"

"It is a good morning, Mark. I may go birding this afternoon after the sea smoke burns off. However, right now I need to register my car. I have my mileage when you're ready," Harriet rumbled.

Keith had made his escape from Harriet and was having a chat with the town administrator.

"Honestly, Keith, I think the best thing to do is behave as we always do. Send the animal control guys out there like we do for every animal related incident," Frank Toothacher said. "If we do some thing different, that will attract attention."

Frank frowned slightly as he spoke to Keith's back, while the selectman peered at Harriet.

Keith turned to look at Frank.

"I don't want another embarrassment plastered all over the papers." Keith turned back to watching Harriet.

Frank mentally sighed. "Before we call an emergency meeting of the selectboard, we first need to have the situation assessed. What killed the moose? How big is it? We need to engage in data collection as our first step," he said.

Keith turned and walked back to Frank's desk.

"You're right. We need to assess the situation. I'll let Mark know he should have Scott or Gaige report directly to me before doing anything else. Good idea."

Keith continued standing in front of Frank's desk

for several minutes.

Puzzled, Frank asked, "Is there anything else I can help you with?"

Keith rocked on his heels and picked up a paperweight from Frank's desk.

"No, not at the moment." Still holding the paperweight, Keith moved back to the office door and continued to peer at Harriet.

As soon as Harriet left, Keith hustled over to the Mark. Looking toward the door, he plopped the paperweigh on the counter. "Mark, when you call the animal control officers, let them know they are to report their findings directly to me right away," Keith said.

"All right," Mark said slowly.

With that, Keith walked with purpose back to his office.

***

As soon as Keith left Mark's counter, Mark called Scott and then Gaige.

"Gaige? This is Mark. We've got a dead moose in Birch Point at Lottie Day's. Keith wants you to report your findings to him before you do anything. I just got off the phone with Scott and he's on his way. I think this will take both of you."

"A dead moose? It's going to take more than just two of us. May need a tow truck. What's Ms. Day's address? I'm heading in that direction now."

***

When the call came in on the dead moose to Sheriff Vimal (Vim) Daggett, he had been enjoying the morning sitting in a secluded spot along Hill Road. He really did have a reason for sitting there. The folks living along Hill Road had been complaining that motorcycles had been racing up and down the curvy, hilly stretch between Fosters Point Road and Berry's Mill Road. When Mark had called him, Vim decided to finish his lunch before heading down to Birch Point to deal with a nasty dead moose.

***

As Scott arrived at Lottie's the sun was beginning to burn off the morning haze. His truck tires crunched over the packed dirt and stone of Lottie's driveway as he parked next to her sedan. He scanned the front yard before walking on to the stoop and knocking.

"Come in; it's open."

Scott pulled the screen door open.

"Hi. I'm Scott. Mark called and said you had a moose down?"

"It's out to the dooryard." Lottie walked down the hall. Her hand beckoned impatiently in the air to indicate that Scott should come in.

Together they moved down the dim hallway and stopped at the kitchen door. The large moose was visible just outside of the tree line.

"Is it dead?" Lottie asked.

Scott pulled gloves out of his back pocket and walked onto the narrow deck. "Can't tell from here. I'll just go down and take a look."

Inching slowly toward the motionless moose, Scott continued to scan the tree line for other animals. As he got closer, he noticed an acrid smell. Squatting down about six feet from the animal, he could just detect the rise and fall of its lungs. He moved back to the deck.

"Still breathing," he said. "Looks like the black flies have been having a feast on its hide."

Lottie pursed her lips and shook her head.

"Poor thing. Can you get it out of my dooryard?"

"Not alone. Someone else should be here soon. We'll figure out what to do when he gets here."

Scott started back to examine the moose. Turning back to Lottie, he said, "I'm going to check further into the woods to see if I can determine what happened to it. The other animal control officer should be here soon. Let him know where I am."

Scott headed toward the woods, stopping to more closely examine the moose. He noted twigs and leaves with what appeared to be vomit on its snout. Scott leaned over the moose. A willow branch was tangled near the moose's ear and he noticed the leaves had a funny sheen. Scott plucked it from the moose. The route the moose had taken was clear. Scott moved into the woods along the path ending at the willow tree.

"Ayuh. It laid down right here and this is where it threw up," he thought.

Scott moved closer to the willow tree. It was

eating this. He looked at the leaves and twig in his hand and back at the tree. The tree had the same faint acidic odor as the moose. Most of the lower limbs had been stripped of their leaves. Scott saw the empty container and tongs lying on the ground, but dismissed them. He twisted one of the limbs off the tree.

***

The moose twitched spasmodically. Snorting violently, he rolled onto his belly. Hungry. With his massive head wobbling on its neck, he cast about looking for food. There. The moose's head tilted as the pressure of his stare fell on Lottie.

Lurching to his feet, the Moose took an unsteady step toward her.

Lottie stumbled up the steps to the deck, keeping her focus on the moose. He locked his dark eyes on Lottie and took another tentative step forward.

Lottie reached the kitchen door.

"Mister, the moose is alive," she rasped, before closing the door behind her. From the safety of her kitchen, she watched the moose drop to the ground as his legs buckled under the quaking barrel of his body.

The scent faded and the moose cast about again.

Hungry. Turning his head toward the woods, the moose caught scent of Scott. Still not in full control of his body, the moose struggled to regain his feet. Snorting, he could tell food was getting closer. Hungry. It managed to remain standing inspite of his wobbling legs. Ears twitching, he listened to Scott's approach. As

Zombie Moose

Scott neared the edge of the woods, the moose moved toward him. Long spindly legs seemed to lag behind the massive barrel of his body as the moose rushed at Scott. No longer concerned about being exposed to danger, all the moose wanted to do was feed.

Scott rolled the twigs and leaves in his hand. This shouldn't have made the moose ill, he thought. Better have a vet look at these.

Scott was still looking down at the leaves in his hand when he was broadsided; the bones in his chest cracking audibly at the force of the impact. Before he could utter a sound, the moose had crushed Scott's head with a dinner-plate-sized hoof.

Lottie's screams spilled out of the house as she watched the moose stomp Scott to death. No longer capable of coherent thought, she stood rooted to the spot as her panicked cries escalated. She moved trembling hands to her mouth in an effort to stop the noise before the evil standing in her yard came for her.

The moose snorted. This wasn't want he wanted. Thrusting his head around searching for a scent, he lurched back into the coolness of the woods, no longer afflicted by black flies.

Chapter 5

Lottie's screams had reduced to gasping sobs when Gaige pulled up behind Scott's truck.

The big oil truck squeezed in the driveway. The still air enveloped Gaige as he slid out of the cab and stood in the driveway. Even though the yard was filled with plants that should attract song birds, it was silence that greeted him. An intermittent croaking from the house made its way to him.

"Hello? Scott?"

He was greeted with stillness. "Scott?"

Gaige felt eyes on him. An uncomfortable feeling of being scrutinized swept over him again. He turned toward the trees, instinctively looking for the source of the inspection. Shivering, he turned back toward the house. The guttural croaking from inside sounded again. He walked up to the door and knocked.

Lottie did not hear him. She stood rooted to the linoleum floor.

Zombie Moose

Casting a wary glance at the tree line, Gaige raised his hand to knock again.

Some mechanism in Lottie chose that moment to flee. Thundering up the hallway she threw herself out the front door and bounced off a stunned Gaige.

"Whoa! Hold on there! What's wrong?"

Gaige attempted to help Lottie to her feet.

She fought against him as only an old lady could.

"Run! Run for your life! Satan is in the woods!"

Gaige tightened his hold. He turned and glanced back at Scott's truck.

"Where is the other animal control officer?"

Squirming and twisting, Lottie tore herself from Gaige's hands.

"Run! It will kill us all! Run!"

From just within the tree line, the moose watched. He had determined the smell was like the other food. Not what he wanted.

Lottie, with adrenalin induced speed, bolted for the road; fear continuing to drive her short, thick legs forward. The moose, staying hidden inside the tree line, followed Lottie as she ran. Again, the smell of this food was wrong. He paused, sniffing the air. Not here. He lurched back into the thick woods, disappearing into the gloom.

Gaige looked back at Scott's truck, Lottie's screams no longer heard. He lingered at the front door, considering whether or not it would accomplish anything to follow Lottie.

"Can't catch her now."

Making a slow turn, he searched for the other animal control officer.

"Scott, you here?"

Continuing to scan the tree line, Gaige moved with caution to the back of the house. A dark shape marred the otherwise picture-perfect lawn. Fear moved from his gut to his throat.

Moving toward the heap with halting steps, he whispered, "Scott?"

Before he reached the mound, Gaige's knees buckled causing him to fall. Pieces of sharply angled bone and bloody chunks of gray and pink matter pushed through what was left of the man's scalp and face. Gaige reeled in horror as he surveyed the flat, two-dimensional pulp that remained of the head. Brain fluid plastered hair in places it should not be. Gaige struggled to his feet. Fighting to control his gagging, he forced himself closer to the body before his legs gave out again.

He avoided looking at the ravaged head and moved to the lifeless hands as he scanned for a wedding ring. When Scott proposed to his wife all he had was a cigar band. His wife was so taken with the gesture that she had rings made to look like cigar bands. Scott's wedding ring was on his hand.

"Oh, Scott." Gaige's head was spinning. He tried to crawl away from the body, but his arms and legs no longer had any strength. Pulling into a fetal position, he lay next to Scott, sobbing.

His eyes kept going back to his friend's hands. Through his tears, he realized that something was clutched in Scott's right hand. Bracing himself up on his hands and knees, he looked more carefully. Despite the overwhelming revulsion Gaige felt, the scientist in him could not help but notice that Scott had been holding a leaf covered twig when he died. Fighting the sickness rising in his throat, he pried open the dead fingers to reveal what appeared to be willow leaves.

Puzzled, Gaige looked around for the tree. The color and feel of them were wrong. He placed them in his shirt pocket as the scream of sirens intruded into his thoughts.

Chapter 6

After running from Gaige, Lottie sought safety in the middle of the road. She continued to call a warning as she caught a breath between screams.

"Dead! We'll all be dead! Satan walks the earth in the form of a moose!"

The retired neighbors and stay-at-home parents living along Birch Point Road were always ready for something exciting to happen. They stepped out of their houses as Lottie ran by. Some even came as far as the road. Cell phones were taken out of pockets and calls were made to alert neighbors on up the road. Mainers love parades, even if it was just Lottie Day.

Lottie had just turned north on Campbell Pond Road, confining herself to the middle. The folks standing in front of their houses were cheering as she ran by. Sheriff Dagget had turned off Berry's Mill Road and noted the people waiting in front of their homes. Seeing the old woman running toward him, he turned on his siren and lights. People cheered and applauded. He pulled sideways across the road and stepped out of the car. Unseeing, Lottie continued to thunder toward him.

"Ma'am, stop!" he shouted.

The mad woman with smears of whoopie pie filling in her gray hair seemed to gain an awareness of Vim's proximity. She thrust out claw like hands and fixed her gaze on him.

He pulled out a Taser.

"Stop!" he ordered.

Lottie did not stop. He looked nervously at the people lining the road as they watched him, then back at the elderly woman who had picked up speed and was sprinting toward him. He put the Taser away and planted himself like a linebacker.

The ensuing collision did not disappoint the spectators. Lottie slammed into the officer then attempted to climb over him onto the cruiser. Vim tried to hold onto the tiny woman with only partial success. Finally, he spun around and held her by pushing her down on the hood of the cruiser.

With arms and legs still flying, Lottie screamed, "Save your children! Satan is coming for them! The demon has taken the form of a moose and is going to kill us all! He's dead. He was just the first to be taken. Satan is coming for your children!"

"Ma'am, you need to calm down and let me help. I'm the police. Dead? Who's dead?" Vim shouted.

"Run! We need to run!" Lottie screamed.

The crowd of spectators had grown. Vim struggled for a few moments and then began to scan the crowd. His eye's landed on Owen Bacon, a volunteer firefighter and lobsterman. "Owen, give me a hand here," Vim shouted as he motioned for him to come forward. As the crowd cheered, the two men got the wriggling Lottie into the back of the cruiser. Confined safely, she continued to pound ineffectively on the windows.

Owen hustled around to the passenger side of the cruiser and climbed in. Vim thought about making him get out, but after one look at Lottie, he decided to let Owen stay.

"Best buckle up," he said to a grinning Owen.

"Ma'am, I need you to calm down and tell me what's going on," Vim said. Seeing that she just continued to rant about Satan, he picked up his microphone.

"I've got a woman, looks to be about sixty, says people are being killed by a demon moose. She was running down the middle of the road screaming about Satan. I think it may have something to do with the downed moose in Birch Point. Send an ambulance out to the Birch Point address. I need to check this out."

Spectators ran for cars to follow Vim in case there was more excitement. The closer they got to Lottie's house, the more agitated she became.

Owen turned to listen to Lottie's raving. The

caravan following Vim's cruiser was now blocking the road.

Pulling around the oil truck, Vim scanned the front lawn. Making sure Lottie was safe in the car, he moved to the back of the house, closely followed by Owen. He stepped back and pulled his gun when he saw the body. "Owen, you stay put," Wide-eyed, Owen nodded and reached for his cell phone.

Gaige was squatting near Scott's body with his head in his hands.

"Sir, you need to step back from the body."

Gaige looked up with eyes filled with tears as he said, "Scott. He's dead."

The officer glanced at the body. He moved to Gaige and helped him to his feet as he spoke into his microphone. "I've got a body here. Guess the woman was right. She was saying it was a moose. Head's been crushed by something. We've got a real crime scene here."

He paused, glancing at Gaige.

"Better send three ambulances."

Lottie was cowering in the back of the cruiser. Even though her voice was nearly gone, she continued to gasp out her warning.

"Run."

Chapter 7

Vim had put Owen in charge of keeping the road clear of spectators so the ambulances could get through. Owen had marshalled other volunteer firefighters who were working crowd control. Emergency vehicle were slowly making their way back to Lottie's house.

Lottie had no interest in leaving the back seat of the cruiser. Beth Grohs and Cole Harrington, the paramedics, had been trying unsuccessfully to get Lottie out. They had attempted to reason with her, but on some level, she knew she was safe where she was.

"Ms. Day, you need to get out of the car and let us help you," Beth said. She tried to pry the door open and Lottie just pulled it shut again.

"Run, run for your life! Satan walks among us!" she screamed.

Cole pulled out his phone. "Doc, this is Cole Harrington. Beth and I have been trying to get Ms. Day out of the cruiser but she's not budging. We think we might need to sedate her," he said. "How much of that should we use? Oh, okay. Thanks."

Beth looked at Cole.

"I don't like doing this the hard way. We can't come at her directly. We need to sneak up on her. You distract her and I'll give her the sedative from the other side."

"I don't know. She's pretty wiry for an old lady," Cole said. They both looked at the wildeyed Lottie. "And just how am I going to distract her?"

"She likes talking about Satan. Just ask her about that. Get her attention long enough for me to sneak in from the other side."

Cole leaned down and looked into the car. He turned to shoot a pleading look at Beth. "Ma'am, are you certain it was Satan? Could it have been

--" Cole glanced over at Beth for help, "could it have been um, you know, a wolfman?

Lottie paused as thought patterns fell into place. Her eyes made contact with Cole as she licked her lips. Beth moved to the other side of the car.

"We need to make certain it wasn't some other type of monster. Are you certain it was Satan? It could have been a wolfman from your description. All hairy and such."

Lottie's head turn slightly as Beth pulled up on the door handle, causing it to click. "We need to be sure it wasn't Bigfoot. They say he's huge and hairy," Cole said quickly.

Lottie's eyes refocused on Cole. "You just never really know with monsters. It might just be a plain old monster, and not Satan at all.

Lottie exclaimed, "No. It wasn't a wolfman or Bigfoot. It was Satan."

"Well, we need to be sure that it was actually Satan. It might have been one of his demons," Cole warmed to his story. "You know demons are easier to deal with than Satan himself. Doesn't Satan usually send his demons first as kind of a foreshadowing of his coming presence?"

Lottie's mouth dropped open as she considered this. Cole's words would ring in her head for many days. Beth moved in with the sedative.

Lottie spun when she felt the prick of the needle and whispered, "Run," as she slumped into Beth's arms.

The mood of the spectators lining the road in front of Lottie's house was no longer one of reveling. Abutting neighbors and more enterprising onlookers who went into the woods for a better look were spreading the news about a body. In a surprisingly short period of time, news crews appeared, wielding cameras and microphones. A scramble for the best vantage point was beginning to boil over into fisticuffs.

The rumor had spread quickly that Satan had taken someone's soul in Lottie Day's dooryard. Cell phones and cameras were ready to get a photograph of the Prince of Darkness.

Gaige's head tilted to one side, eyebrows drawn together, as he tried to listen to Vim. His eyes shifted to the erupting chaos going on around him.

"It's like a hurricane and I'm at the center," he thought to himself. "I know this. I've been here before."

"Mr. LaRoche? Mr. LaRoche do you understand my question?"

Gaige's vision shifted back to Vim. "What? Sorry, could you repeat that?"

Vim looked closely at Gaige. "Did you see what killed —" Gaige's eyes went to the ambulance as they loaded Scott's body.

"No, I'm sorry. I got here too late." His eyes continued to watch the ambulance as his eyebrows pulled together again.

"Ms. Day saw it." He looked at Vim. "Said it was Satan."

"Mr. LaRoche, I'm going to have one of the EMTs take a look at you. You stay put."

A potbellied man with thinning steel-gray hair made his way to Gaige as soon as Vim left.

"Horrible. Just horrible," the man said.

Gaige looked up.

"Oh hello, Keith. I didn't see a moose."

Keith's nose became redder than it was.

"Right. You didn't see what happened."

"You know, I think everyone has asked me that question today. Must be important."

Gaige scanned the crowd,

"Looks to be enough people here for a [12]town meeting. Why don't we put it to a vote?"

Keith crossed his arms on his chest and frowned. "Important!" Keith blustered, "Gaige, you do know that someone died here. It was an accident, right?"

Gaige turned to watch the ambulance carrying Scott's body negotiate the driveway lined with gawpers.

Keith's long face was now completely red. "Gaige, I understand you saw the incident."

"Nope. Can't say that I did," Gaige said.

"Well, you were the official on site when it occurred," Keith said. "Can you tell me what kind of animal it was? You know these rumors are just flying. Something about Satan stealing souls and a monster eating people's brains," Keith chuckled.

"No, I didn't see what happened. Scott was dead when I arrived. You need to ask Ms. Day. She saw it."

"Urm. Ms. Day. Yes. Are you certain you saw nothing? No vicious monster killing people? Mark said it was a moose call, not a huge rampaging brain-eating demon."

Gaige rubbed his forehead and looked at the sweat on his hand before wiping it on his shirt. As his hand paused over his shirt pocket, he felt the leaves. I need to look at these, he thought. He stood up and

---

12   **Town Meetings**: A town meeting in Maine is a volatile event that either erupts into a full-scale caged death match or bores everyone to death.

walked away.

"Gaige, where are you going? You're the animal control officer here. You need to report on what happened."

Gaige's eyes focused for the first time since finding Scott. He stopped moving and turned to a florid Keith.

With a flat voice, Gaige said, "Keith, I don't know what you want me to say. I didn't see anything. No animal, no monster, nothing. There was a large area where something had been lying down near Scott's body, but I didn't see anything."

Gaige glanced over at the oil truck.

"I need to call my dispatcher. I have deliveries to make. If you don't like it, you can fire me."

Cole walked up just as Gaige stalked away from Keith.

"Mr. LaRoche, I need to take a look at you. Let's move over here," Cole pointed to the ambulance.

"I've got stuff to do," Gaige said.

Cole looked at the truck and nodded. "Why don't you give your dispatcher a call and get another driver out here. I don't want you driving until a doctor has a chance to check you out."

"And what? You going to arrest me?"

Cole said, "Nope. I don't arrest people. I just try to keep them alive."

He gestured toward the sheriff's cruiser. "I'm sure they will have questions for you. Me, I just want to check your vitals." He nodded toward the ambulance. "Shall we?"

Keith stepped between Cole and Gaige.

"I need to find out what happened. You'll have to wait."

Cole looked at Keith. "I'm sorry. I need to get him checked out. If you interfere with that I will get the sheriff over here to remove you."

"But," Keith sputtered, "I'm a selectman!"

"And my cat eats spaghetti," Cole said. He placed his hand under Gaige's arm and led him gently to the ambulance. "This fellow is in shock."

Gaige had not been paying attention to what Cole was asking. He hardly noticed Cole taking vitals. Gaige had responded, but would not be able to tell anyone later what was asked, or how he answered. His brain was already cataloguing the facts that he knew. Absently, he pilfered some plastic bags to put samples in, along with rubber gloves from the ambulance.

Cole grew concerned at the distracted way in which Gaige was behaving. He seemed to be answering all the questions and his vitals looked good, but he seemed strangely distant. "I want you to go to the hospital and let them take a good look at you."

Gaige looked past Cole's shoulder at the tree line.

"At the very least, give your dispatcher a call and take the rest of the day off."

Gaige looked toward the oil truck.

"Okay."

Zombie Moose

Keith had been watching Cole work on Gaige.

As soon as Cole finished, Keith followed Gaige to the oil truck. Concerned, Cole watched Keith make his move and motioned toward Vim.

Chapter 8

Vim nodded at Cole and went to Keith.

"Sir, I'm going to have to ask you to move behind the barrier."

"But I'm the chair of the selectboard. I need people to see me here."

"Keith, I know who you are. We'll let you know something when we do. This is a crime scene, and we need people to stay out of the way until we finish with it."

"Vim, you don't understand." Keith's arm swept out toward the crowd lining the road. "This could create a panic. I need to do the job these fine folks [13]elected me to do."

Vim looked at the crowd. "Well then, why don't you go over there and calm down the citizens who

---

13   **Selectmen's Job**: Frank Toothacher was doing the job the good people of West Bath had elected Keith to do. Keith was too busy being too big for his britches.

elected you? That would be an appropriate job for a selectman."

Keith's eyes hardened. "Son, my job here is to get the facts and let people know that someone they trust is in charge," he snapped.

Vim shifted his stance and placed his hands on his equipment belt, his eyes locked on Keith.

"Really?"

Keith glanced at Vim's gun and smiled.

"Son, I'm not trying to work at cross purposes to you law enforcement folks. I just want to make certain wild rumors aren't flying around that might cause a panic in our little town." His hand gestured toward the crowd. "No telling what might happen."

Vim didn't say a word. Keith stepped closer, putting his hand on Vim's shoulder. Vim glared at him.

Keith's nose turned bright red again while the color leached into the rest of his face.

"Come on Vim, we can't have people spreading rumors thath there's a monster running around in West Bath," he barked angrily.

"Well, Mr. Selectman, we don't know anything yet. When we do, we'll put out the facts, not speculation," Vim said as he turned toward Gaige.

"Stay away from Gaige until he gets some time to rest. The guy is in shock. It's going to catch up with him; he needs to get some downtime. You need to give it to him."

"Keeping these good people safe and calm is

more important. We need to let them know it isn't a monster we're dealing with."

The muscles in Vim's jaw tightened.

"Whether it was an animal, a man, a space alien or hell spawn, whoever did this was a monster."

Keith sputtered.

Vim looked around the front lawn and pointed to a young man with a notebook standing on the edge of the neighbor's yard.

"A reporter from the Coastal Journal is there. Why don't you go and spin things to him?"

With a momentary panicked look in the direction Vim was pointing, Keith noted the reporter and several camera crews. He said between clenched teeth, "I have the luck of [14]Hiram Smith." Without a backward glance, he plastered a smile on his face and hurried to the journalist.

---

14   **Hiram Smith**: participated in the 1836-1839 war with England over Maine's northern boundary. He was the only man to die in that war. We don't know what killed him, but it wasn't because he was shot. Therefore, when you are wicked unlucky in New England, you are said to have the luck of Hiram Smith.

Chapter 9

Quinn had been listening to the police scanner at her desk. She knew something bad was going on at Lottie Day's and that someone had died. She knew several ambulances were needed. Photos had even started showing up online. She had tried to contact Gaige, but he wasn't answering. When he called for the dispatcher, she nearly jumped out of her skin. She grabbed the radio.

"Gaige, are you okay?"

"Quinn, that animal control call I went on," Gaige's voice broke, "The police are here and they won't let me go. You need to get someone to come get the truck." Gaige looked at the traffic blocking the street. "Don't know if you can get it out yet. Crowd's pretty big."

"Gaige! I've been listening to the police scanner. I thought it might be you who was killed. You weren't answering when I called," Quinn said.

"Sure, we'll get someone out there right away to get the truck."

"Scott's dead," Gaige choked out, "his head was crushed."

Quinn glanced at the pictures on her monitor. "Scott? It was Scott? Oh no. Okay. All right. You need someone to drive you someplace?"

"I'm not sure they'll let me go," Gaige leaned against the truck door. "Cole told me to take the rest of the day off."

"At the very least," Quinn said, "I'm going to get another driver then we'll be on our way to you. Stay put."

Gaige hung up the microphone and looked at Mrs. Menard's cookies on the seat beside him.

He watched the crowd behind the flimsy police barrier and the journalists who were marking their territories. His gut tightened. He picked up the ancient cookies and flung them from the truck cab.

"I can't do this again."

The cookies clattered across nearby vehicles, one of the treats struck Beth.

Rubbing her shoulder where the petrified cookie had hit her, Beth turned to look for her assailant. She saw Gaige slumped over the truck's steering wheel and ran to him.

"Sir, how are you doing?"

Gaige turned his tear filled eyes to Beth, who had now opened the truck door.

"Sir, do you need some help?"

Gaige looked away from her, struggling to compose himself.

"Are you going to be keeping me any longer, or can I go with the new driver?" he said.

"Let me take a quick look at you, then we'll see if the sheriff needs you any longer," she said.

She took his pulse. "This has been a pretty rough day for you," she said. "We could take you to the hospital in an ambulance."

Gaige thought about how they loaded Scott into the ambulance and drove him away.

"No. There's someone coming to get me," he said.

"Well, have them take you to the hospital. I'm going to call ahead and let them know you're coming," Beth ordered.

A sudden wave of weariness swept over Gaige. Getting a sedative and sleeping for the rest of the day didn't sound so bad. He needed to get away from the growing ranks of reporters at the scene.

Beth was watching him carefully. "You just sit right here." She closed the door. "I'll see if the sheriff needs you here any longer. I'll be right back," she assured him.

Beth approached Vim, who was keeping a close eye on Keith. "Officer, the man who found the body is in the fuel oil truck cab. He doesn't appear to be doing so well. I'd like to send him to the hospital if you're done with him," Beth said.

"Gaige?" Vim looked at the truck.

"I think it's just shock. But I'd like him to see a doctor and get something to relax him. He's got someone on the way to pick him up."

Vim moved toward the truck with Beth following. Gaige was lying down in the seat.

Vim opened the truck door and nodded. "I think we can let you go for now. You need to see the doctor. Stay in the area for a few days in case we have any questions."

Gaige grunted in response.

The sheriff's microphone crackled out, "We've got another crushed body on Fosters Point Road."

Wide-eyed, Gaige sat up. He noticed Keith running toward the road.

Gaige was no longer exhausted, and the scuttling reporters no longer caused him concern. Something is wrong. I need to figure this out.

Vim spoke into his microphone as he hurried off, "Owen, get the road open now."

Beth noted the renewed energy in Gaige as he reached to put the key in the ignition. She placed a hand on his arm.

"Whoa! Sir, you need to wait for your ride and go to the hospital."

Chapter 10

"Didn't I tell them that tourists were here already? And here they are buying my whoopie pies." Walter Ouellette stood up to meet the tourist family stopping at his roadside [15]whoopie pie stand.

"Can I help you folks?"

"Yes. How much for your cake things?" the mother asked.

"Well, that depends. You want the original chocolate or--"

Walter stopped as his eyes caught sight of the moose standing just inside the tree line. The man who was snapping photographs of Walter turned to see what he was staring at.

"Don't see that everyday. That there, my friends,

---

15   **Roadside Stands**: A pickup truck pulled off at a wide spot with several coolers, a lawn chair with an umbrella, lots of bug spray, whatever is in season – including decorative holiday wreaths or lobsters, directions for lost tourists, and participating in unofficial sign competitions.

is a moose. Don't see them out in the open too often."

The moose ambled slowly out of the woods, stopping just short of the roadside opposite Walter's truck.

The tourists were delighted and the father adjusted the camera, rapidly clicking off photos. The little girl cowered behind her mother as she peered wide eyed at the huge animal with the spindly legs. The man moved cautiously across the road toward the moose, snapping photographs as he walked.

"Look! It's just standing there. Come here and I'll take your picture with it."

His daughter cowered further behind her mother.

"Ralph, get back here!" his wife snapped.

Walter moved to the rear of his pickup truck. "Young fellow, that's a wild animal there and looks to weigh nearly a ton and a half. Don't spook it."

Ralph waved away the old man's warning and continued towards the moose who observed the approach of the tourist.

"Hungry. So hungry."

It sniffed the air, looking towards Walter then back to the man slowly approaching.

"Different."

The man came within a few feet of the moose.

"See. Perfectly safe," he turned, grinning towards his family. "I heard you can walk right up to these things."

The moose snorted as it sampled the air again.

Zombie Moose

"Hungry."

Seeming to be tangled in his own legs, it moved towards the tourist with surprising speed.

Walter was transfixed as streams of sweat poured down his back. The scene unfolded in slow motion. Walter's mouth opened, but no sound issued from it. He watched, helpless, as the moose slammed into the tourist with a sickening crunch and then trampled him.

It was the sound of screaming that caught Walter's attention. He realized that is wasn't his screaming he was hearing. Jerking from his fixation on the moose to the hysterical woman and child, he grabbed them by the arms, and forced the two of them into the cab of his truck. Walter had one foot in the cab as he realized he had left his phone on his toppled lawn chair. With bile rising in his throat at the sight of the moose eating the man's brains, Walter put his foot back on the ground.

Closing the truck's door to ensure that the woman and child were safe, Walter walked slowly towards his phone. The moose flicked his ears but made no other movement as it continued to gobble chunks of brain. Walter took two more steps and stretched to grab the cell phone. Pausing to look once again at the moose, he moved towards the safety of the truck.

In the blink of an eye, the moose was across the road; his crushing weight pressed Walter against the truck. Unable to draw enough breath to scream, Walter nearly suffocated in the moose's acrid stench.

The animal's gore-covered maw brushed against Walter, leaving bloody bits of brain tissue dangling from the brim of his ball cap. The moose breathed deeply.

"Not food."

Snorting, he tossed his head before walking into the woods.

Stunning darkness closed in around Walter. When the police arrived, they found him crumpled on the ground with the woman sobbing over her husband's body.

"Sir? Sir? Are you okay?"

Walter's eyes fluttered open and, with a jolt of fear, he lurched away from Cole, the first paramedic on the scene. Walter scrambled backward, screaming as his head swiveled around looking for the moose.

"Sir, it's all right. You're safe. The police are here," Cole said.

Walter focused on Cole.

"He killed that man. Just knocked him down and killed him. Then he ate the man's brains before it came for me." Walter squinted at Cole. "Who are you?"

"My name's Cole. I'm here to help you. That fellow over there is the sheriff. He wants to ask you some questions. I'm going to help you sit in your chair. Let's get you up."

"Where's the woman and the child?" Panicked, Walter looked around.

"They're safe. She called 911. You put them in the truck," Cole said, "You're a hero."

Cole helped Walter to his feet and guided him to his lawn chair. He then motioned for Vim to come over.

"Sir, this is Sheriff Daggett. He wants to ask you a few questions then we're going to take you to the hospital to have a doctor take a look at you."

Walter scanned the tree line. "I don't need any hospital. I need to get away from that killer moose. It could be anywhere."

Vim nodded. "I understand that you saw a moose kill a man."

"[16]Ayuh. It killed that man right enough," Walter shuddered. "Ate his brains too."

Walter pulled off his cap and looked at the bloody brain matter on the brim. Pulling a handkerchief from his back pocket, he rubbed his face with a trembling hand before [17]wiping his hat on the grass and placing it back on his head.

"Nearly crushed me, it did. Just pushed me right into the truck and stared hard at me before it left. Didn't act like any moose I ever saw."

***

"Look, you can't block off Fosters Point. There are people living here. How will they get to the town office?"

---

16   **Ayuh**: Maine affirmative. When pronounced properly, it identifies you as a Mainer. When mangled, it identifies you as being from away and open to ridicule.

17   No Mainer would waste a perfectly good hat.

Vim turned to look at Keith.

"Don't you live on Fosters Point? You didn't complain when we blocked off roads on the Berry's Mill side."

"That was different. There was a huge crowd," Keith protested.

Vim's face turned toward the blue sky as he extended his hand, palm up, toward the growing throng gathering between [18]Witch Spring Road and Bull Rock Road.

Ignoring Vim's gesture, Keith continued. "It's important for the town hall to be accessible so they can give out the correct information. The safety of the citizenry is at stake. The town hall is a symbol of the [19]rule of law!"

"Ah. So you think people can't call and talk to Frank? Or maybe Hill Road just disappeared? Or is it so people driving by on Witch Spring Road won't notice the scene of the murder? Keith, we're closing the road. People can go around." Vim pointed at Walter's truck. "Why aren't you more concerned about the fact that two people in West Bath are dead at the hands of unknown persons or," Vim paused, "moose?"

Sputtering, Keith said, "I am concerned. I just

18   **Witch Spring Road**: Road running through West Bath that connects Bath and Brunswick. Renamed State Road by the state of Maine.

19   **Town Office**: Symbol of where you pay your car registration and dog license, hold committee meetings and a hangout for the selectmen.

don't want to create a panic with misinformation."

Vim sneered at Keith. "This is a police investigation. We may not get many homicides or animals that kill people, but we are trained to handle them. Why don't you go push some state paperwork around? Isn't that what you do?"

Keith grabbed Vim's arm. "This is an overreach of your authority! It's an abuse of power. You're escalating the situation unnecessarily."

Vim stiffened and lifted his hand in caution.

Keith immediately released Vim's arm and retreated from under his scrutiny.

"Well, if you will excuse me, I've got to ensure the safety of the citizens of West Bath." Vim looked back at Witch Spring Road and spoke into his microphone. "Right. We've got some traffic backing up here at New Meadows and Witch Spring. Can we get someone for traffic control at that intersection?"

Frowning, Keith wiped the sweat from his face. "Can we at least tone down the activity here?"

"My Aunt Fanny's doilies, Keith. Within the hour, we've had two people get their heads crushed and all you're worried about is how to spin this? It's a crime scene. You can't tone down a crime scene." Vim spat on the ground.

Keith watched Vim stalk away as he felt any semblance of control slip away from him. His eyes pivoted towards Witch Spring Road. Cars were indeed slowing down or pulling off to get a better look at the action. Keith swallowed hard. He needed to regain control. His stomach was in knots even before he spotted the television van threading its way down Fosters Point Road. He reached for his cell phone, but it slipped out of his sweaty hand and back into his pocket.

As if his words alone could cause the phone to comply with his demand he stated, "I am the chair of the selectboard!" With that declaration, he jerked the phone from his pocket.

"Frank, you need to get down here and get a handle on this situation now," Keith barked into the phone.

"Keith, is that you? What situation? Where?"
"These" Keith paused as he followed the progress of the television van.

"This situation with" Keith began to whisper into the phone, "this Lottie Day thing."

The town office had not yet been [20]notified of the death of Scott or the incident at Walter's whoopie pie stand. Frank was confused.

"The downed moose?"

"Shhh. Don't use the word, moose, you fool. And for heaven's sake don't mention anything about Satan! Good thing crazy old Ms. Day is in the hospital under sedation. Put out a press release saying that

20   Keith had gone out to Lottie's to "be in charge" of clearing out the dead moose. No one had alerted Frank or Mark that someone had been killed. As often happens, the town office is the last to know.

I'm assisting the police in their investigations. Don't mention anything about monsters, Satan, or a brain-eating zombie. The reporters are almost here. Just say it was an isolated wild animal attack."

Frank was even more confused and decided that Keith had one too many at lunch with the boys. "What? Lottie's in the hospital? Satan? Zombies?" Frank said.

"Are you a complete idiot?" Keith watched the television van find a parking spot. "I'm here at the end of Fosters Point by Bull Rock. Get a press release out immediately stating that I'm in charge of the situation and everything is under control."

"What are you talking about? Did something happen with the moose?"

"You are an idiot. I've got to go. I need to talk with the reporters. Just get that taken care of. Tell anyone who calls it isn't a brain-eating moose." Keith ended the call.

Keith moved to the camera crew as they were organizing themselves. He plastered a practiced smile on his face and held out his hand. "Hello, I'm Keith Neves, chairman of the selectboard here in West Bath." A man untangling some power cords glanced at Keith before returning his attention to his work. The plastic smile was still radiating from Keith as the reporters walked right past him to Walter's truck. "Did I mention that I'm chairman of the selectboard?" Keith shouted after them.

***

Frank stared at the phone.

"Mark, find out what's going on with the moose at Lottie Day's and whatever is going on down at Bull Rock Road. Keith just called and he was more incoherent than usual. Have we heard from Scott or Gaige yet?"

Mark nodded and made a couple of calls.

"Lord, have mercy." He turned to the computer.

"Frank, you're going to want to see this. Looks like two people have been killed. There's already pictures posted online. Most are saying it was a moose that eats brains or some sort of demon."

Frank watched as Mark pulled up photo after photo.

"I'm heading down to Bull Rock. I'll let you know more when I get there," Frank said.

He paused at the door, "Might want to call in some of the volunteers to help with the phones. Tell people we are cooperating with the police investigations and there will be more information later."

Chapter 11

When Quinn arrived with Sam, the crowd had thinned considerably. News had spread rapidly that Satan was now over on Fosters Point Road and everyone wanted to get a selfie with the Dark Prince. There were enough people remaining at the first site that Quinn and Sam had to park and hike down to Lottie's house.

Most of the time, Quinn didn't mind her small stature. She jumped up and down a couple of times in an attempt to see what was happening.

"I can't see a thing, Sam. There are too many people. We should be getting close now. Can you see anything?"

Sam rolled up onto the balls of his feet and stretched.

"Ayuh. Flashy lights right up ahead."

They wriggled through the crowd until they reached Lottie's driveway. The large oil truck was in plain sight. They ducked under the police tape.

"Hey, you two, stop."

Quinn looked over the top of her glasses at the man barring their way.

"Owen, what are you doing here?"

"I should be saying the same to you," Owen said.

"Sam's here to finish Gaige's route and I'm here to take Gaige home," Quinn said.

Owen glanced at the oil truck.

"Let me make sure it's okay with everyone first."

Quinn and Sam started for the truck as soon as Owen walked away. When they reached it, Sam opened the door. Gaige was sitting in the cab with his head back and his eyes closed.

"Are you okay? This is horrible,"

Quinn glanced at the emergency vehicles.

Gaige turned toward the sound of Quinn's voice. He rubbed his eyes and blinked.

Quinn peered over the top of her glasses at Gaige.

"You okay? You don't look so good."

"How do you expect me to be? Scott's dead. Look, we need to go over to Fosters Point."

Sam frowned at Quinn and stretched his neck to look into the truck.

"Gaige, are the keys in the truck?" he asked.

Gaige focused on Sam and nodded.

"Under the driver's side visor."

Gaige looked at the road.

"Don't think you can get out yet."
Gaige turned his attention back to Quinn.
"Where's your car?"
"Back about a quarter mile," Quinn said.
Gaige was pale and his eyes were seriously red.
"Gaige, you need to go someplace and rest."
Gaige all but fell out of the truck and had to steady himself on Sam.

"Buddy, go take a rest. You're all wobbly," Sam said.

"No, I'm okay. I need to find out what's going on here. Let's go," Gaige said.

Sam patted Gaige on the shoulder and climbed into the truck.

"Are you certain you want to go to Fosters Point? It's probably just as crowded there as it is here," Quinn said.

Gaige looked toward the woods.
"No. I need more samples."
"Samples of what? What are you up to?" Quinn asked.

Gaige pulled the bag of twigs and leaves from his pocket.

Alarmed, Quinn scanned the area and hissed, "You are removing evidence from a crime scene! You do understand that you're tampering with a crime scene. I don't need to become your accomplice."
"I took these before the police arrived."
Quinn swatted at his hand.

"Put that away," Quinn said.

"Quinn, you going to be okay?" Sam asked.

Gaige placed the bagged twigs and leaves back in his pocket.

Quinn glared at Gaige.

"I'll be fine, Sam. Thanks for taking the rest of the route."

Gaige was already heading for the road and Quinn had to run to catch up with him.

"I need to get more samples before I can determine what happened. Scott isn't the only one dead. There's another one over near Bull Rock. Let's go."

Quinn put out her hand to stop him.

"Gaige, I really think –"

"You were supposed to wait over there. Quinn, this is a crime scene. You can't go walking all over," Owen said.

Gaige frowned at Owen and walked around Quinn as she attempted to block his way.

"Let's go."

Quinn looked down at the [21]shoes on her feet.

"I am so glad I'm not wearing heels."

---

21   **Sturdy Shoes**: Sturdy shoes are vital to Mainers due to long winters and a boot-sucking mud season. The shoe stores tend to be just as serious. J.L.Coombs was a shoe store in Maine that sold sturdy brands of shoes. They had a commercial jingle that included the line, "If you don't like my shoes, then to hell with you." I don't think they're in business anymore.

Zombie Moose

✳✳✳

"Where's the car?" Gaige barked.

When they reached Quinn's vehicle Gaige nearly fell into the passenger seat.

"Gaige, just look at yourself, you're barely standing. You can go back to Fosters Point later," Quinn said.

Gaige was drumming his knees with his hands and listening to the police scanner in Quinn's car. "No. I want to know what happened. They said

it was a moose." He sat up. "Moose don't eat people."

Quinn frowned, "No. That is really strange." Glancing over at Gaige, Quinn saw the determination in his face. "Okay, but then we go to the hospital. Deal?"

"Sure. Park on Bull Rock," he ordered.

She looked at the crowd blocking the road. "I heard that Walter got some pictures on his phone."

Gaige looked around.

"Was it a moose?"

Quinn frowned, bit her upper lip and nodded her head.

She said, "I don't believe it either. Estimates are that it was about a ton and a half. The tourists had a digital camera as well, but the police have that all as evidence."

"I need to see those pictures. Something has to be wrong with that moose."

Quinn shook her head.

"It's evidence now."

Gaige's red-rimmed eyes closed.

"Sorry, Gaige. Scott was a friend. I don't mean to be —" she paused peering at Gaige. He had opened the door and turned to exit the car.

"You going to be okay?"

"Yep. Give me a minute here," he said as he steadied himself. "I'm fine. Go."

Quinn touched his arm.

"You want some help?"

"I'm okay. We're here. Take some pictures of the attack site if you can get close enough."

Gaige straightened up.

"Go ahead," he said as he flicked his hand toward the crowd.

Quinn retrieved her camera from the back seat and disappeared into the crowd. Gaige studied the tree line. He assured himself that he had some empty bags on him. Taking a deep breath, he walked unsteadily into the stand of trees just behind the area the police had roped off.

When Quinn returned, Gaige was still gone. She waited and reviewed the shots she had taken. Gaige still had not arrived. She spun around looking for him in the crowd. I should have stayed with him. He's in shock. Just as she was about to go back to look for him along Fosters Point, she spotted him. He was quickly stepping out of the trees with the assistance of a police officer.

"Gaige! Are you okay?"

"You know this guy?" the officer said.

"Ayuh. He's in shock. He was the first one on the scene over at Ms. Days."

The officer looked at Gaige.

"Uh-huh. First on the scene at Birch Point. Your name is what? And why are you here?"

Gaige gave the officer his name and address.

"I got a guy over here who claims to have been at Birch Point. Names Gaige LaRoche," the officer said into his microphone.

The microphone crackled, Vim's voice could be heard. "Gaige is here? He was at the first site. He's not a suspect. Send him to the hospital."

The officer glared at Gaige.

"Go home or go to the hospital. Stay out of our crime scene."

The officer turned to look at Quinn.

"Get him out of here. Now."

Quinn put her arm around Gaige. "Well, that worked out well," Quinn complained. "Nearly got yourself arrested. I think you need to take the officer's advice," she said as she steered him toward the car.

Gaige grunted as she settled him in the passenger seat.

Quinn pursed her lips and rubbed the bridge of her nose.

"All right. Folks are saying that both Walter and

the tourist lady saw the moose standing in the woods watching the whoopie pie stand."

Gaige focused on Quinn.

"Really?"

"Just knocked the tourist down and crushed his head." Quinn wrinkled her nose.

"They said the moose was eating his brains. And they both watched it happening. The moose crossed the road and even smashed Walter against his truck before leaving. I think this is a first; [22]Walter and Lottie agreeing on anything."

Quinn looked over at the crowded scene and back to Gaige as he put the keys in the ignition.

"Home or hospital?"

"No, not yet."

Gaige scanned the trees again.

"The moose didn't kill Walter and it could have."

Gaige scanned the tree line and started pulling bags full of vegetation from his pockets.

"You didn't take —" Quinn looked at Gaige.

He wasn't listening to her. He was frowning at the reporters clustering around Keith as they pulled away.

"Gaige, this is kind of like it was before. You need to be careful."

Gaige stopped sorting through the small bags

22   Walter and Lottie always made town meetings entertaining. They not only disagreed on everything, they did it loudly and while hurling insults at one another. Most folks just came to watch as the fur flew between these two old adversaries.

and looked over at her.

"I'm not a kid anymore. I know what I'm doing."

He swept his hand toward the crowd.

"They don't. They think that if it is a moose they can kill it and the problem is solved. What if this isn't isolated to this moose? We need to get to the cause."

Quinn pushed her glasses up on her nose.

"Gaige, you're the biologist. Why would a moose eat brains?"

Gaige studied the tree line.

"I don't know."

He looked around at the growing mob of onlookers gathering at the end of Fosters Point.

"I'm going to find out."

"Gaige, stay out of this. It's more than some clam flats in danger here. We've got a one ton-killer running around out there."

Frowning, Gaige looked back down at his samples.

"Quinn, did you get to talk to any of the witnesses?"

"Nope. I did talk with some of the folks standing around though."

"Do you know where he headed?"

Quinn blinked at Gaige.

"Boy, you are delirious. This is a crime scene now. You can't go wandering around in it. You almost got arrested back there," Quinn's said.

"I know. Where else was the moose that isn't a

part of the crime scene?"

"No place."

"Where was the moose, Quinn?" he demanded.

Quinn looked at the police around them.

"This

isn't about making building contractors angry. You could get yourself killed. Do you understand that?"

Gaige stared at Quinn.

Quinn said, "Right. Okay. They said it came out of the woods here," Quinn tilted her head toward the tree line, "Then went into the woods over there behind the New Meadows Inn."

Gaige placed the samples back in his pocket. "Okay. Let's go over there."

Quinn put the key in the ignition and said, "All right. I'll take you over to the Inn. You can look around over there. I'll honk if I see anyone coming. Be careful, we don't know where that thing is. As big as they are, moose can hide really well."

She watched him walk into the woods as she turned up the scanner.

Gaige moved unsteadily toward the second spot Quinn had indicated. Walking into the woods, he stopped at some freshly broken vegetation. Looking down he noted the plate-sized moose prints.

Standing up, he scanned the surrounding trees. "Bingo."

Gaige broke a small twig that had a clump of fur clinging to it.

Zombie Moose

"Just what I was looking for."

Chapter 12

Gaige stumbled from the woods at the place where he had entered and made his way back to Quinn's car. He could hear the police scanner popping as he approached. He put his hands on the vehicle's roof to steady himself and leaned in the window.

"I need to see those photographs that Walter and the tourists took."

"Gaige, it's evidence; already bagged and tagged."

"Quinn, I'm worried about this. A moose is a very shy herbivore. Something besides rutting made it attack people. I need to identify the cause before more animals start doing the same thing. It almost sounds like the moose was stalking the tourists."

Quinn looked at Gaige.

"Oh man, I know that look. I thought you were trying to put your past behind you so you could get a job. Remember? No more crusades. That clam flat thing is still following you around."

Frowning, Gaige turned and looked at the growing throng of cars filling the parking lot and spilling onto Witch Spring Road.

"Quinn, I don't think the moose is here any longer. It's moved on. There are too many people here. It may not even be in West Bath now," he said.

He straightened up and walked a few unsteady steps towards the New Meadows River.

Quinn exited the car and followed him. Quinn glared at Gaige.

"Gaige, don't."

"Ms. Day's description was not very accurate, but she did say it was a moose. I should talk to Walter."

Gaige turned from his contemplation of the river.

"I need those photographs."

"Gaige, listen to yourself," Quinn cautioned.

"Come on, Quinn. We both know that moose don't attack and eat people."

"Ms. Day talks nonsense most of the time," Quinn said.

"Yet two people have been killed in the same way. Walter and Ms. Day actually agree that it was a moose."

Gaige turned and walked toward Fosters Point.

"Gaige!"

Quinn's eyes narrowed as Gaige headed toward the crowd.

"Don't do something dumb," she called ineffectively.

Quinn shook her head as Gaige disappeared into

the crowd of onlookers.

"Like that's going to happen," Quinn muttered.

She looked at the river before walking back to her vehicle.

"Gaige is right. The river is at low tide. The moose could easily have crossed unseen into Brunswick."

Quinn pulled her camera from the backseat and walked back to the water. She took pictures of the river and the area around the New Meadows Inn, including the tree line.

Quinn's police scanner crackled.

"-- that selectman and the town administrator are not helping us here. They won't stay away from the crime scene and they're interfering. We have our hands full with this posse that's forming up. There's talk about heading out to kill the moose. This trigger happy mob will shoot anything that moves, including a school bus."

The scanner continued to pop.

"On my way. Let Keith know if they're still hanging around when I get there, I'm going to arrest them for interfering with a police investigation. Let them know that I'll make certain the television crews get some footage of them being handcuffed. That should clear the politicians out. Not so confident about controlling the hunters." Quinn shook her head and turned to the woods again. Frowning, she thought, Could be anywhere. This is a [23]wicked pissah.

---

23   **Wicked Pissah**: Multipurpose New England term that

Chapter 13

Art and Ethel Suiter had been coming to Maine with their children during the summer months for decades. This year would be their last camping trip. In the beginning, the family came to visit for just a week or two. Now that the children were grown and they were retired, the couple arrived at the end of May. They stayed at the same campground in their Airstream until the fall colors faded.

The moose made its way toward familiar territory down at Birch Point. The hunger gnawing at its belly was growing more and more insistent. Instead of heading for a safe resting place, the moose made its way to an area it remembered.

The spot was in the open, full of people and noise. Turning east, the moose moved through heavily

---

can mean something really over-the-top good or really bad. Here Quinn is using the term in the latter sense. Context is everything.

wooded terrain in the direction of the campground.

It was quiet, the blaring of the sirens muted by distance. The moose sniffed the air. There was food here.

"Ethel, listen to the scanner. Sounds like big doings." Art said.

"I'm not deaf. I can hear the sirens. Been going off most the afternoon. Anyone said what's going on?" Ethel said.

"Seems a couple of folks have been killed."

Ethel turned to Art in alarm.

"Oh, dear me.

That's horrible. How did it happen?"

"I'm not really certain, but I think they're saying it was a moose."

"A moose? I didn't know moose were dangerous. Are there any moose in this area? I've never seen one here," Ethel exclaimed.

"Sounds like they may be organizing a hunt. Think I'll drive up and check it out. Might be able to see the moose. Want to come?"

The old man grabbed the keys off the hook beside the camper door.

"Think I do. I'm not wanting to stay here by myself with a killer moose on the loose."

Ethel considered the interior of the camper.

"I need some groceries anyway. Let me finish sweeping up first," Ethel said.

"Well, don't take too long. I don't want to miss

anything. Think I'll text the kids and let them know."

Ethel rolled her eyes and continued sweeping.

The moose moved toward the southwest corner of the campground.

Art and Ethel weren't going to miss a thing.

***

The moose watched the campground. As he sampled the air, he knew he had hit the jackpot. He watched as a crew of landscapers arrived on the scene pulling trailers. The moose remained still as the landscapers moved lawn mowers off the trailers and drove them down to where the moose waited. It considered these new arrivals.

"Not food."

The sounds of the lawnmowers and weed-eaters caused the moose's ears to twitch, but the thought of food drove him forward. He stepped out of the woods.

The mowers froze as the moose made his way toward them. Being Mainers, they understood this was a unique opportunity, since moose rarely show themselves. Of course, they pulled out cell phones and started snapping pictures.

As the moose got closer, one of the mowers noticed the blood on the animal's maw.

"Hold up, fellas. I think this moose might be sick. Best stay back!" he shouted.

The moose's attention was drawn to the man closest to him. He walked to within three feet of the nearest mower. The mower could clearly see the blood and flesh clinging to the moose's mouth. Slowly extending its bloody muzzle, he sniffed the man and snorted.

"Different."

He moved away from the mower as the man's knees collapsed and he fell to the ground.

Campers also noted the moose's arrival and a temporary excitement spread across the campground. Art stepped out of the Airstream with Ethel following closely behind. Art was in time to see the moose knock down a camper and crush his head. He turned quickly, shoving Ethel back inside the trailer.

"The killer moose is here," he said as he locked the door.

Her eye's huge, Ethel pulled back the curtain. The couple watched the moose stomp around the camp killing and eating their friends.

Art, with his eyes locked on the horrific scene unfolding before him, dialed 911. When the operator answered.

"He's here and he'll kill us all," Art said.

"Sir, where are you and what is there?"

"The moose. It's eating Jimmy's brains right now."

Ethel turned to throw up in the little sink.

The 911 operator motioned to the other operators.

"Sir, where are you right now?"

"Um, we're at the campground here in Phippsburg down Meadowbrook Road."

Zombie Moose

"Okay, sir, are you out in the open?"

"No, me and the wife are in the trailer."

"Okay. I'm going to stay on the line with you. Stay inside. I've got the sheriff on the way."

Art watched the moose ram a pop-up trailer.

"I don't know if that's a good idea," Art said.

"Sir, stay put. Help is on the way."

The moose tore the fabric away from the popup camper.

"Whoever you send, it won't be quick enough."

Chapter 14

Gaige made his way to the police barrier blocking Fosters Point. The gawkers were starting to lose interest, but enough were still hanging around that Gaige wasn't able to get to the front of the crowd. He loitered in the back of the group.

Keith was also standing at the back edge of the crowd. He spotted Gaige and marched over to him.

"What are you doing here? Trying to stir things up? Aren't you supposed to be at the hospital or something?" Keith snapped.

"Keith, we've got to do something here. This isn't right."

"What isn't right?"

Keith's piggy eyes locked on Gaige.

"There's no proof that it's a moose. And if it is some wild animal then we need to kill it immediately. That's what's right."

"Look, Keith, even you have to admit that moose

don't behave like that. We need to find out what's wrong with it."

Gaige looked around at the number of people with rifles.

"We don't need it killed."

Keith moved in close to Gaige and hissed.

"You don't know what you're talking about. Wrong with it? We need to kill it as soon as possible? Do you even have a shred of scientific proof? Huh? Speak up, Clam Boy."

Keith stabbed a finger at Gaige.

Gaige shifted backwards, away from Keith.

"Just as I thought. You don't know anything. Well, Mr. Clam Flat, you can count the Town of West Bath out of any of your wacko plans. If you try to bring us into your environmental fantasy, the town will sue."

Gaige dropped his eyes.

"It might have something that's contagious or it might be a mutation. We need to find what caused this behavior. There might be more moose out there who will behave the same way."

"Contagious!"

Keith looked around to make certain that no one was eavesdropping.

"You're just making guesses now. Look here. You're lucky you have a job as an animal control officer in West Bath. I don't see anyone lining up to hire you as a biologist. You had better stay out of this before everyone in the county knows what kind of kook you are. I'm sure you don't want to spend the rest of your life delivering fuel oil." Keith laughed. "Now that is funny. The environmental wacko delivering fuel oil."

Keith stopped laughing and eyed Gaige.

"If you pull any kind of stunt, Clam Boy, I'll make certain that you can't even work doing that. Now get out of here before I fire you."

Keith spun around, pulled his cell phone from his pocket and headed toward his car.

Gaige stared after him. His head was spinning and he felt numb. The fog must be rolling in.

Everything is so soft and gray, Gaige thought. Somewhere far away he heard Vim threatening the crowd by telling them he would arrest anyone who formed a militia.

Quinn had gone looking for Gaige when she noticed the crowd had gathered around something.

In the center of the circle of people, Gaige was lying on the ground and Cole was kneeling beside him.

"What happened? Is he okay?"

Quinn tried to push through to Gaige.

Cole looked up.

"He's okay. He passed out. He should already be at the hospital."

He turned back to Gaige.

"Gaige? Gaige look at me."

Gaige's gaze swam over to the voice.

"Gaige, do you know who I am?"

"Yeah, you're that paramedic."

Cole nodded. "That's good. We're going to take you to the hospital now."

"I've got a ride already."

Cole looked back at Quinn. "That doesn't seem to have worked out so well. I think we'll just take you there. Think you can walk?"

Cole wrapped his arm around Gaige's waist and helped him to his feet. Someone threw a blanket over Gaige's shoulders.

"Come on, buddy. Lean on me. This way."

Quinn ran for her car, jumped in, and follow the ambulance to the hospital. She was almost there when the chatter on the scanner reported the attack at the campground. The report stated that an unknown number of people had been killed by a moose. She could feel fear rise in her chest.

"This thing is moving fast. I've got to warn people."

Quinn pulled over to the side of the road and grabbed her laptop from the back seat. She pulled the card out of her camera and uploaded the photographs.

"This is bad", she thought. "What if Gaige is right and it's contagious?"

Her hands hovered over the keyboard.

"I've got to let people know they're in danger."

Chapter 15

The blood of conquerors ran in Idalene Richie's veins.

Not royalty or anything cool like that.

However, Idalene's progenitor had gained a place of honor among the other Vikings because of his skill at berserking. Sure, every Viking could berserk – even old ladies – but the guy at the beginning of Idalene's family tree was a berserker's berserker. Everyone wanted him along on a raid or pillage as long as he was in front of the group. When he let go with a berserk and was in full blood rage, he was indiscriminate in where he landed his axe. He was an equal opportunity hatchet man. The rest of the Vikings knew to stay well out of his range.

Throughout generations, the violent plundering traits of her Nordic ancestors had been diluted and had all but disappeared from her family. Even the physical characteristics of height, strength, and blonde coloring only cropped up occasionally. Idalene's Viking genes stayed true to the orignals.

Her five-foot, ten-inch height, body strength, and aggressive nature made her a natural for basketball.

She had been awarded a full athletic scholarship and everyone thought she would go professional. Idalene had even considered it at one point, but had rejected this career path in the end because it had a limited lifespan.

While she was still in high school, she won a number of local and state beauty pageants. Idalene had grown into a statuesque, blue-eyed Valkyrie by the time she was 16 years old. Her pale golden blonde hair reflected sunlight in a way that most women only dreamed about. Her complexion and facial features were such that she was stunning without makeup.

When she walked into a room, like her seafaring ancestors landing on a foreign shore, she conquered it.

While she chafed at the restrictions placed on her before and after she had won the beauty contests, that wasn't what made her decide not to follow this career path. She knew it wouldn't bring her the power she craved. Idalene wanted to conquer entire governments and worked towards equipping herself to do just that.

Her progress toward this goal made a huge leap forward during her sophomore year in college.

While a prelaw student at the University of Maine, she became involved in an environmental dispute. At first she cast her lot with the environmentalists because of the positive publicity they were gaining. She soon realized that the ragtag group of high school students did not have the wherewithall to defeat a well-funded group of developers.

When she was approached by a lawyer who represented the developers, she cut a deal to ensure a clear path for her to achieve her goals.

Without a second thought or twinge of regret, she sold out the teenaged environmentalists and erased any connection she had to them.

The developers, showing their appreciation for her cutthroat skills, guided her path through school and internships until she found herself, in her late twenties, as the Chief of Staff for the current governor of Maine. Idalene was actively positioning herself to move to the next level.

Staffers who blocked her way, whether it was in the elevator or on a project, were fired shortly after each incident.

Not that Idalene ever had a direct hand in the termination of a staffer, but it always happened. As a survival trait, government employees with any sense tended to cut a clear path when Idalene approached.

When Idalene glided into her office the morning of the killings, she read the reports left for her by Polly Malloy, her assistant.

Idalene had hired Polly based on her mousy appearance, not on the superior clerical skills she possessed. The selection was soley to allow Idalene to make a visual statement of her dominance and Polly was the perfect physical counterpoint. When Idalene marched into a room with the very forgettable Polly scuttling behind carrying a load of documentation, it only emphasized Idalene's underlying power.

Now, she turned her attention to her emails. She had received a message inviting her to a meeting with the strongest senatorial candidate later in the week. Her full red lips curled into a smile as she accepted the invitation.

The call from the state police came to Polly's desk in the late afternoon. There had been three documented moose attacks in a little town in midcoast Maine. Polly immediately verified the information and printed out police reports. She read through them quickly, highlighting pertinent data before going into Idalene's office.

Knocking on the door, she waited for Idalene to respond.

"Yes?"

Polly opened the door.

"Excuse me, Ms. Richie, but there seems to have been some trouble down the coast."

Idalene frowned and looked at the clock.

Polly continued, "A moose has been attacking and killing people in West Bath."

Polly could sense Idalene's full attention focused on her and her throat tightened.

"There were three locations. We're still getting

numbers from the last one, which was a tourist campground."

Idalene's right eyebrow rose slightly as she stuck out her well-manicured hand for the paperwork Polly held.

Idalene read the reports.

"Get me a map of the West Bath area and find me someone to talk to who's in charge there. Now," Idalene ordered.

Polly turned and fled.

Idalene went back to reading the report. She paused and tapped the paper with a perfect red fingernail.

"So we meet again," she said, smiling. Idalene always loved a good battle, especially when the odds were stacked in her favor.

She pressed the intercom button on her phone.

"Polly, find me moose experts and get them over here now. Have some food delivered from that deli and get the governor on the line. Bring me everything you can find on Gaige LaRoche. Have you found anyone in charge in West Bath yet?"

***

Idalene pulled on her jacket and walked down the hall to the governor's office. Her head was spinning. At last count, six people had died. This was a disaster. They needed to do something fast. It was complicated by LaRoche, but she had handled him before and she could do it again. Problem was she wasn't certain yet how best to control the killer moose story.

As she walked past staff, she smiled with confidence and exchanged greetings. Her brain was working overtime.

"We've got to get a handle on this right away. We need to find the moose and kill it," she thought.

She nodded at the governor's administrative assistant, Velda, and walked into the governor's office.

"Governor Pelletier, I'm sure you've seen the initial reports on whatever it is that's happening in West Bath."

The governor looked up at Idalene.

"Ms. Richie, this is terrible. Those poor people."

"Yes, Governor, it is terrible."

"We've got to do something. Call a press conference or something."

Idalene put on her most concerned look. She shook her head slowly.

"Governor, the first thing you need to do is contact the families of those unfortunate folks who were killed in this as of yet unidentified disaster."

"But it was a moose."

Idalene smiled slightly.

"That is just what some of those folks down there are saying. We have no confirmation it was a moose. Could have been anything," Idalene's brain clicked into place and she smiled more broadly, "including bad clams."

"Oh," the governor looked confused, "it was bad

clams?"

"We're not certain yet."

"Do bad clams make your head implode?"

Idalene tilted her head to the side as she considered the governor's comment.

"We're not certain about that yet either. We're having our best people look into it. Meanwhile, I recommend we call an emergency meeting of all state department heads and work on a strategy," her eyes narrowed slightly, "to protect the people of the great state of Maine."

"Excellent idea."

"I'll have Polly give Velda contact numbers for the family members of the deceased. Velda can start calling them so you can express your condolences. I'll send over a script for you to read."

"Okay. I feel better already. Thanks again, Ms. Richie; you always know what to do."

"Just serving the people of this great state. You should probably call West Bath and offer support in this time of crisis. I'll let Velda know to call an immediate meeting."

Idalene walked back to her office. She now had the beginnings of a plan.

Chapter 16

"Go to bed now. The doc said you could go home only if you rest and someone stays with you," Quinn scolded.

"Just let me put my samples in the fridge," Gaige fussed.

"Give them to me; I'll do it." Quinn held out her hand.

"I want to reduce contamination. I'll just —"

"You already have them bagged up, right?"

Quinn put her hand on Gaige's chest, and he stumbled backwards. She grabbed his shoulder to steady him.

"Look at you; you're barely standing. Give them to me," she said.

Gaige hesitated. He did appreciate Quinn allowing him to stay at her place and knew he needed to sleep.

Quinn grimaced.

"I'm not going to throw them out. I'm going to put them in the fridge. I promise."

Emptying his pockets, he said, "All right, make certain that you —"

"Gaige, I'm just putting them in the fridge. You can start your mad scientist experiments tomorrow. Go to bed," Quinn ordered.

Gaige lowered his eyes. He was bone weary. It would be wise to get some sleep and come at it fresh. He turned and stumbled into the guest bedroom. He was asleep before his head hit the pillow.

Frowning, Quinn gathered up the various baggies containing Gaige's collection of pilfered samples. She took a close look at the hair sample. Wrinkling her nose, she carried the lot into the kitchen.

***

Gaige was awake shortly after 2:00 a.m.

Disoriented, he kicked and thrashed at the estraining covers. Nightmares of reporters with microphones crowding him until he was suffocating still lingered around the edges of his consciousness.

He sat up on the edge of the bed wiping the sweat from his face. Images from the previous day marched in front of his closed eyes. Reporters and Lottie Day's screams seemed to be in every corner of his recollections.

He remembered the emotional wounds left from another time when he had had his very first encounter with the press. In the beginning, it had appeared the press was an ally, but Gaige's naïveté only made him fodder for the news cycle.

When the tide turned against him, it didn't take the media long to become a pack of vicious predators. After they had finished tearing him apart, they had turned on his family.

It didn't matter that it was lies that made the press become his enemies. All that mattered was grabbing the headline first. In the aftermath, his mother had lost her job at the environmental firm where she worked and Gaige had lost all respect from the scientific community he had hoped to join.

It wasn't that Gaige was a poor scientist or even an undisciplined one like his instructors thought. In fact, he was probably one of the brightest stars among his peers. The biggest problem with Gaige was he was able to see beyond the conventional wisdom of his profession to visualize all the possibilities. He could make the intuitive leap to understanding.

It irritated some of his teachers that he was able to find the answer without going through all the steps. After his very public fall from grace as a result of his shoreline development protest, those educators felt their opinion of him was justified.

What hurt him during the clam flat protest was his inability to predict the darker side of ambition, or to pay attention to the more underhanded nuances of human nature. This made him an easy target for an aggressively career-oriented pre-law student during his efforts to save a clam flat. It had puzzled him that public opinion had turned against him.

At the time, he didn't realize it was a friendly face that had planted the knife until after it was all said and done.

Since that incident, Gaige had worked hard to keep a low profile. Every college, except one, rejected his application. By some miracle, he was accepted into the University of Maine system and managed to graduate.

Yader Johnson, the chair of the science department, thought Gaige was using science to showboat and had a keen dislike for him. The general air of distrust and open disdain trickled down through most of the professors and finally to his fellow students. Operating under these handicaps Gaige was never able to distinguish himself.

He graduated in the low side of the middle of the pack. And then there was the lab accident that prevented him from pursuing his doctorate. Between the false news stories and his unremarkable college career, he ended up taking the only job he could find, delivering fuel oil. Even then, it was Quinn who gave him the job at the fuel oil company.

"I can't do this again," he whispered into the darkness.

Rubbing his face, his dark thoughts returned to Lottie Day's door yard. Sobbing, he buried his face in Quinn's lavender scented pillow as he mourned the loss of one of his few friends.

In the darkness of the predawn, Gaige had a moment of clarity. Gaige knew Keith was right. The moose needed to die. It was up to him to kill it and avenge Scott's death. Once the moose was dead, he would fade into the shadows again. Gaige often entertained thoughts of moving to the west coast or Canada. He could move to Washington or Oregon and start over. He had even seriously considered changing his name.

Gaige washed his face and silently made his way downstairs to the room where Quinn's grandfather kept his gun collection. Pulling out the Winchester 308 Coyote and some ammo, he went outside and hid the gun in the bushes. Next, he walked to the fuel oil company where he retrieved his vehicle then drove back to Quinn's house to pick up the weapon.

He pulled a map out of the glove box and opened it on the seat beside him. After a few moments, he thumped it.

"I bet that sucker is down around Birch Point," he said, "Probably right about here."

It was just beginning to lighten up on the eastern horizon, but not enough to clearly distinguish objects, when Gaige had made his way deep into the woods. The flashlight he was using to find his way in the bramble proved to be an annoyance as he was constantly swatting at mosquitoes and black flies. He held the light in his mouth to free up a hand to shoo away his little tormentors. Slogging through the wet, swampy terrain only stirred up an increasingly large swarm of the pests.

He stopped moving forward when he realized the mosquitoes and black flies had disappeared. In fact, he no longer heard the rustling of small nocturnal animals around him. That's when he felt warm breath on his neck infused with an acrid odor. Turning slowly, he found himself six inches from a massive wall of fur. The clumped hair on the maw of the beast was stiff with what looked like dried blood and globules of flesh. Looking up into the eyes of the animal, Gaige dropped the gun and froze.

Chapter 17

The moose pushed his muzzle forward and touched it against Gaige's forehead. It snorted, blowing mucus on Gaige's face, hair, and clothes.

Gaige didn't breathe.

The moose backed up a step and hung his head down to examine the dropped gun. He looked back at Gaige and snorted again before turning around. He moved a few steps and folded his legs in slow motion. Settling into a sleeping position, the moose took one last look at Gaige before closing his eyes and going to sleep.

Terror held Gaige rooted to the spot. His eyes shifted again and again to find the gun lying somewhere at his feet but his limbs would not respond. His arms and legs trembled violently. The flashlight had fallen and landed light side down. Gaige cast about for it. With rapid, jerky movements, he all but fell trying to retrieve the light from the muck at his feet. Grabbing the light, he scanned the ground for the gun.

It was the overwhelming acrid stench that led him back to sanity. Logic set in and took notice of what was happening. He paused, his hand hovering over the gun.

"Why am I alive?" he asked himself.

He aimed the flashlight at the moose's snout.

"Can't be certain if that's blood, but your snout is matted with something."

Other than being covered with mucus, Gaige was unharmed. Puzzled, he considered the moose.

"Why didn't you attack?" he said.

The moose's only response was to twitch one of his furry ears.

"You don't even care that I'm here. Not the behavior I would expect from a moose. Something isn't right with you."

Gaige moved a few feet from the moose and continued to examine him. His hide contained healing sores that were consistent with black fly bites. The strange thing was there didn't appear to be any new sores.

"What is it that's making you attack people? And why aren't the flies bothering you?"

Gaige looked around.

"Why aren't they bothering me? And what is that smell? It's everywhere."

Gaige sniffed at the mucus dripping from his sleeve.

"Ayuh. Everywhere."

He carefully pulled off his mucus-covered shirt, using it to collect the snot from his face and hair.

He gently pulled his pants off to protect his new samples before he stooped to pick up the gun.

The moose's ears twitched at the sounds, but he remained asleep.

Gaige stood mulling over this new information as the sun rose.

"You need to stay hidden until I can figure this out."

Turning, Gaige walked out of the clearing back to his car.

Chapter 18

Quinn was angry when she found Gaige and one of her grandfather's guns were gone. Unfortunately for Gaige, he answered his cell phone when she called.

Since Quinn had a few things to say to Gaige, she decided to go to his apartment and explain things to him up close and personal. She was pacing in front of his door when he arrived.

"Gaige, where's Grandpa's gun?"

Gaige pointed to the car.

Quinn peered into the vehicle.

"You thief!"

She pulled open the car door and pointed to the muck-covered gun.

"What? You took my grandfather's gun just to dump it in the mud?"

She grabbed the soiled gun.

"I'm one of the few friends you have left, and you thought it was a good idea to steal from me?"

She walked up to him and stopped in her tracks.
 "What is that smell?"
"Exactly!"
"No. I mean," Quinn leaned into Gaige and sniffed, "you stink."
She realized he was standing in front of her in just his boxers.
"Why are you nearly naked?"
"I'm serious. I need to find out why I stink."
Quinn's mouth dropped open.
"I don't know where you've been, but" waiving her hand in front of her face, she said, "you're going to need to burn your clothes."
Quinn's shoulders relaxed. She recalled how hard it had been for Gaige as a college student after the reporters had ripped him apart. Watching the power they exerted against an innocent, well-meaning kid had been a valuable education for her. Now, she was beginning to worry about his sanity.
"Gaige, are you doing all right? You don't seem to be thinking clearly."
"I wasn't all right, but I am now. I found the moose," Gaige said, "walked right up to the place he was bedded down. I was just six inches away from him. We just stood there and looked at each other."
"Then why aren't you dead?"
Gaige grabbed Quinn's shoulders and grinned.
 "Exactly. I meant to kill it, but I wasn't really expecting to find him. He scared me pretty bad. He's a

big sucker. Everything we know about him, everything that happened yesterday," he threw his hands up in the air. "I should be dead. He wasn't at all aggressive. He blew a lot of snot all over me."

Quinn's eyes shifted to Gaige's slick hair and her nose wrinkled. "How do you know he was THE moose?"

"It looked like there was blood and what might have been brain tissue all over his snout, and he smelled bad. Not just regular moose bad. He stunk to high heaven. The odd thing is there were no blackflies or mosquitoes either. We were in the deep woods and there were no insects."

Gaige paused as his thoughts were distracted by the volume of new information he had collected while observing the moose.

Quinn waited as she recognized he was thinking.

Suddenly, Gaige's eyes refocused on her.

"And," Gaige smiled at Quinn. "He got bored and then went back to sleep. It was weird. He wasn't even bothered that I was there."

He paused again and mumbled.

"The smell wasn't right; I need to find out why."

A soft breeze blew toward Quinn. She backed up and covered her nose.

"Man, you smell really, really bad."

Gaige sniffed his arm.

Still grinning he said, "Well, yes. The smell got my attention right away. Place just reeked of it."

He waived at the air.

"Notice any insects?"

Quinn stood still, listening for the buzz and whine of mosquitos.

Gaige nodded his head.

"See?"

His eyes grew distant.

"The moose wasn't acting like a normal moose. Got to find out what's in this snot before someone kills him. I've got to do it now."

Chapter 19

Idalene prepared for battle. She had been following the moose attacks last evening on news feeds and through social media. By the time she went to bed, she was confident in her ability to handle this blip. She had a flawless plan to cast doubt, confuse facts, and divert attention to LaRoche.

She had decided to wear a simple pastel blue shift coupled with a soft grey cardigan, with her blonde hair loose and pulled back with a matching grey headband to give her an innocent air for the cameras. Her shoes were grey suede ballerinas, her nails clear and her makeup understated. Perfect.

Before leaving for work, she decided to check the news feeds one more time. After all, she didn't want any surprises. Some idiot could have gotten a shot of the moose that the inept police force didn't confiscate. She scanned the various headlines as she drank her coffee. Her mouth fell open as she set down her cup with a thump.

The blog post was well-researched and obviously from someone who was at the first two sites. It linked to the press release issued from the West Bath town office, had sound bites from Keith Neves, the Chair of the West Bath Selectboard, and photographs of the first two sites. It called attention to the vague nature of the press release, the harsh comments by the selectman, and the deadly nature of the attacks by the moose. It discussed how the moose could easily swim over to Brunswick or go into Bath and Phippsburg unseen. The overall article was a clear warning about the attacks.

It ended with a twofold recommendation to avoid wooded areas and seek the shelter of a vehicle or other solid structure if a moose appeared. The anonymous blogger also requested any photographs or video of the killer moose be forwarded to the Sea Smoke email address.

Idalene's eyes were wild. Not only was his blog post lucid, but the blogger also had completely derailed Idalene's plans for spinning the next news cycle. Unlike the information coming from other tweets, blogs, and social media posts, Sea Smoke had gained a reputation for its accuracy, timeliness and longevity. Idalene had even gone to the Sea Smoke site herself in the past to check facts.

She straightened up and considered her clothes. Ugly determination replaced confusion in her blue eyes.

"Nothing has changed. The plan still works. You are just one anonymous coward hiding behind an electronic wall."

She smoothed her perfect hair and glided from her chair.

"I'll crush you, along with everyone else."

***

Idalene walked into the press conference with brisk purpose. She shook the hand of the lackey from Fish and Wildlife and smiled warmly at the gathered reporters. The initial questions came just like she had scripted them. She responded as she had planned.

"We are not certain that it was a moose."

"The police have not released any photographs of the incidents."

"The governor is on the phone as we speak, calling the families of the victims."

"We are examining a number of possible causes."

"Our first duty is to the people of this great state."

Finally, Don Jannings, a journalist working for a small weekly paper asked a real question. Don naively believed it was his job to report the news.

"Ms. Richie, what is being done to safeguard people until you can find the moose?"

"As I stated earlier, it hasn't been determined it is a moose at this point. We have our top people working to isolate the cause. It could be anything. In fact," Idalene allowed her eyes to twinkle, "I have even heard a wild rumor flying around that some bad clams caused this tragedy."

Still operating under the illusion that he should push for the truth, Don said, "We have reports from people who identified a rampaging moose as the cause, not bad clams. In fact, a blog, Sea Smoke, is warning people to stay away from wooded areas. That sounds reasonable under the circumstances. Why haven't we seen similar warnings from the governor's office?"

Idalene smiled indulgently.

"It's Don, isn't it? Well, Don, I would place my trust in trained scientists over uninformed, anonymous bloggers any day," she paused to chuckle. "We can't have unsubstantiated social media gossip dictate how we protect people in Maine. After all, if social media were a reliable source of information, you folks would all be out of work."

Except for the now blushing Don, it was the reporters turn to laugh softly.

"The governor's office is on top of the situation. In fact, I believe he has scheduled a meeting this morning to develop a fact-based strategy. Anything else? No?"

Idalene suppressed a smile. That went perfectly, she thought to herself.

"Okay, who's next?"

Polly was waiting at the door to let Idalene know where the strategy session was and provide her with materials for the meeting.

"We are just starting the tourist season. I don't

care how you do it, but find out who this Sea Smoke blogger is. That is your top priority."

"Put our people on some counter-stories and play up an environmental terrorist angle. Flood the grapevine with the fact that we put no credence in the rumor it was bad clams."

"Do we have bloggers we can influence? If we do, reach out and influence them."

"Meet with the party president to make certain he is informed of our strategy. Squelch the killer moose; play it down in the press. We need to get this resolved before the word gets to the tourists. Make sure this can't be traced back to us. No fingerprints here."

When Polly didn't move immediately, Idalene snapped, "Well, I believe you have work to do. You'd best get to it!"

Idalene snatched the paperwork and brushed past Polly.

"I'm going to the meeting. I expect to have some usable information when I get back."

Polly's fingernails bit into the palms of her hands as she watched Idalene march away.

Chapter 20

Governor Pelletier looked around the table. Frowning, he picked up the report and began to wave it in the air.

"Ladies and gentlemen, we are in crisis; a crisis of a magnitude that demands the full attention of each of us."

He glared at the people sitting in the room and settled on Idalene.

"Ms. Richie, please bring us up to speed on what you know."

Nodding to the governor, Idalene said, "Of course, Governor."

She picked up the paperwork in front of her.

"At approximately 1:30 p.m. yesterday afternoon an animal control officer in West Bath, Scott Anderson, died while responding to a downed moose call."

She flipped through the paperwork and added, "At approximately 3:45 p.m. yesterday a tourist, Hank

Zelman, was attacked and killed. Later that afternoon, a campsite just over the West Bath line in Phippsburg was the site of a third assault. We're still getting information on the people killed there."

"Muddled eyewitness reports mean we have no clear idea of the person or persons responsible. What we do know is Mainers and tourists are being killed."

Idalene dropped a number of photographs on the table. There were a number of gasps.

"Please take a look and pass them around. These pictures are not available to the public as of yet. There are a number of dangerous rumors flying around. These are of grave concern. We need a strategy to deal with these lies so they don't lead to an uncontrolled panic situation."

"We have to get control of this or we will lose the tourist revenue from this season!" said Cindy Thibedeau, the representative from the Chamber of Commerce.

Idalene nodded.

"While our primary focus is the safety of citizens of this great state, tourism is a real concern. Early reports are vague. Eyewitnesses, of course, were in shock and are still being interviewed. We need to use caution as we move forward. For instance, there seems to be a persistent unsubstantiated rumor that the attacks stem from bad clams poached from closed flats. What gives this ridiculous rumor credence is that only one Mainer died. The rest of the victims were from away and therefore, may have been unaware of the dangers of digging clams from closed flats."

Idalene paused to let that information sink in.

"Of course, there is no scientific reason to believe that bad clams would make your head explode."

Idalene sat down.

The governor said, "Any thoughts? Let's start with tourism."

The governor looked around the room.

"I don't see Rachel. Did she get word of the meeting? This crisis impacts her department."

The Governor looked at Idalene.

"Oh, yes, sir. Her father had back surgery. She took a leave of absence to pull lobster traps for him."

Idalene looked toward the end of the table and smiled.

"Dave is here in her place."

The governor's face brightened.

"Excellent. Dave, didn't see you over there. We should grab some coffee after this meeting. Do you have any thoughts on the situation?"

Dave leaned back and placed his hands together.

"What the organizational hierarchy needs to do is avoid going into a crisis management mode and exercise due diligence to create a stable information architecture. Engaging in a blamestorm will only create a time suck with no deliverable outcome. At the end of the day, we should establish best practices in order to fast-track a seamless synergy."

Dave nodded his head and pursed his lips.

"Establish a point person to engage in risk management until such time as all the ducks are in a row and this hiccup can be put to bed."

The governor beamed at Dave.

"Well said, well said. Ms. Richie is point person on implementation of Dave's suggestions. She speaks for me." He looked at Idalene.

"Pull some department heads together and do what Dave just said."

Idalene nodded gravely, "Yes, sir."

One of the attendees leaned over and whispered, "What did that guy just say?" She was greeted with a scowl.

"Weren't you listening? He's brilliant."

"I don't think I've seen that guy before. Who is he?"

"You must be new here. That's Dave Levesque. He's a freelance meeting substitute."

"Say what?"

Polly had slipped in to deliver a message to Idalene and stayed. She waited quietly near the door with her phone's recorder on. When the meeting ended, she approached Idalene and reported the results of her inquiries.

"So the party chair will be at Starbucks at 5:30 p.m., I think you need to stop by there about then and get yourself a mocha latte. And please don't be obvious." Idalene walked away.

Polly waited until the room had cleared. She told the other secretaries who came to clean the room she would handle it. Collecting all the stray paperwork, she went back to the copy room to shred the excess documentation. While she was there, she made digital copies of the photographs.

Chapter 21

Gaige had gone back to Quinn's house to collect his other samples. When he returned to his apartment, he pulled out his lab equipment. He carefully cleaned a work surface in the kitchen. By noon, Gaige was no longer aware of his surroundings.

The phone rang, but went unanswered. A neighbor knocked on the door, but Gaige remained bent over his microscope. It wasn't until the landlady opened his door with her key and walked in that his bleary eyes looked up from his work.

"Young man, I thought I told you not to do that chemical drug stuff here."

She held her nose and pointed at the equipment on the kitchen counter.

"Are you running a meth lab or something? Your eyes are all red." The landlady peered around the apartment and glared at the lab equipment.

"What? No. It's not drugs. It's —"

"The other tenants are complaining about the smell. I know you're up to something. I told you the last time I would evict you if you did that again," she glared at him. "You have a week to get out."

"But —"

"I told you I didn't care what you were making here on these premises. It could be bathtub gin for all I care, it stinks. It annoys the other tenants. You were warned, weirdo. Now you're gone."

She shoved the eviction notice in his hand.

Gaige watched her rocking gait as she waddled away. He noted some of the other tenants were standing outside their doors glaring at him.

Confused, he closed the door and returned to his work.

About 4:00 p.m., Quinn was back, pounding on the door.

"Gaige, are you in there? Are you okay? I have [24]lobster rolls."

Gaige was heating another beaker full of liquid and shouted, "Its open."

"Pew. What are you doing in here?" "Quinn, look at this," Gaige pointed at the microscope. "There's some toxic substance on the leaves. I can't figure out what it is, but it appears to be organic. I think the combination of these willow leaves, black fly venom, and whatever

---

24   **Lobster Roll**: Lobster sandwich. Shoot, in Maine during the summer you can even get a lobster roll at McDonald's.

this substance is, it has something to do with the behavior of the moose. I just can't figure out what it is."

Quinn looked through the microscope at the round and stringy shaped things before looking up at him.

"Okay. Is this why you haven't been answering your phone?"

"Oh, sorry. Was it ringing? I didn't hear it."

Gaige's eyes focused on Quinn.

Quinn walked to the answering machine and hit the play button. Several messages came spilling off the machine, most of them from Quinn.

Gaige frowned.

"Sorry. Really didn't hear them."

Quinn rolled her eyes and shrugged.

"Okay. Tell me about this," she gestured at the kitchen.

"These are samples collected from the two attack sites, and these," he pointed to another stack of slides, "are from my encounter with the moose." Gaige frowned. "This may not be an isolated event. If this substance is tainting the food source for these animals, we may have more aberrant behavior."

Gaige looked at the counter containing his limited equipment. "The good news is, it may be reversible." He picked up a Petri dish. "We've got to find out what this organic substance is before we can work on what will neutralize it."

Quinn looked down at his cramped handwritten

notes and spotted the eviction notice.

"When did you get this?"

"Oh, this morning, I think." Gaige squinted.

"You have a week? And you're okay with this?"

Gaige's eyes seemed to focus on the apartment.

"No." He slumped in the chair.

Quinn passed him a lobster roll.

"Show me what you're talking about. We'll work on the apartment thing later."

Gaige sat up on the chair and his eyes brightened.

"Well, see, there is this substance adhering to the willow leaves that appears to be the same material I found on these moose hairs."

"That you stole from crime scenes."

Gaige frowned.

"Someone had to. Scott had the leaves in his hand and I found moose hair at Ms. Day's and over by Bull Rock Road. And there was some substance at Ms. Day's, either vomit or drool. I need a better lab to find out exactly what it is, but there is a substance there that appears to be organic. I've been trying all day to identify it, but I'm going to need a better lab."

His eyes traveled over to the kitchen counter again.

"So let me get this straight. You removed evidence from an active crime scene, haven't told anyone important, your kitchen lab isn't sufficient to analyze it, and you're not all that concerned about being evicted? It's a good thing you haven't been arrested." Quinn frowned. "But maybe being in jail is your solution to your housing issue."

"Of course, you're right!"

Quinn was incredulous.

"You want to go to jail?"

"No. I need to get a commercial lab."

Gaige wasn't listening to her anymore. He was muttering to himself.

"I need better equipment."

He didn't notice that Quinn was taking photos of his slides, notes and microscope.

Chapter 22

After the department head meeting, Idalene drove directly to West Bath. She told Polly to phone ahead to alert the selectboard that she was on her way. When she arrived, they were all present.

Keith had been watching the parking lot from the town administrator's office. As soon as Idalene's silver Audi pulled in, he all but sprinted for the door of the town offices.

"Ms. Richie, I don't know if you remember me. I'm Keith Neves, chair of the selectboard here in our little town. We met at the training session for selectmen a few years ago," he said.

"Why would I remember you, you little bug. Good thing I reminded Polly to do bios on these idiots," she thought.

Giving Keith her most charming smile, she extended her hand and said, "Why yes, I do remember you. How is your wife, Ellen? That training was excellent, wasn't it? It opened my eyes to the difficult job selectmen choose to take on."

Keith beamed as he shook Idalene's hand.

"Keith, as you know, the reason I'm here today is because of the unfortunate circumstances of yesterday. The governor wishes to ensure everyone in West Bath has what is needed to deal with this crisis. Are the other selectmen here?"

"Oh, yes. They're all inside," Keith stammered.

Idalene waited through a moment of awkward silence while Keith continued to grin at her. She smiled at the adoration in his little squinty eyes.

"Well, Mr. Chairman, you are going to make everything easier than I imagined," she thought.

"Why don't we go inside and get started then?" she purred.

Once they settled themselves around the table, Idalene said, "Is there anything the governor can do for you?"

The selectmen threw out a number of issues. Idalene pretended to take notes. "These are all valid concerns that I will put before the governor, but what I meant was, how he could help during this time of crisis."

Keith, sensitive to the slight undercurrent of frustration in Idalene's voice, took charge of the selectboard.

"Ms. Richie, our plan is simple. Kill the moose. It would be helpful if the governor would declare a special hunting permit for moose in West Bath," Keith said.

The suggestion for a special hunting permit caught Idalene off guard. She, too, had decided the moose must die, sooner, rather than later. However, she had not considered issuing a special permit.

"Our experts have not determined the cause or causes of the incidents that occurred yesterday. There are a number of wild rumors flying around, and we should stick with verified facts."

Idalene chuckled, "There is even one suggestion that bad clams caused the deaths. Imagine bad clams making your head explode!"

Idalene shook her head and chuckled.

"However, I will grant, for argument's sake, that it was a moose. Why would you need a special permit to remove an animal nuisance? Can't animal control take care of it?"

Keith's face turned bright red. Idalene wondered if he was going to have a heart attack. "Hit a cord here," she thought.

"The problem is, one of our animal control officers was killed in the first assault. The other one is —"

Keith turned to look at the other selectmen. Idalene kept her face passive and murmured,

"I read the report. That was so unfortunate. I am sorry for your loss."

Keith blurted out, "The other one is a real

environmental screwball. I don't know that he can be relied upon to kill the moose."

Keith looked at the other selectmen who all nodded in agreement.

"Yesterday he was telling me we shouldn't kill it. He was trying to get me to believe that the animal was sick and may be contagious." Keith snorted, "Thinks he can cure the thing."

Idalene did a mental happy dance. "Ah, I see. Do you think he may be correct and we have a contagion situation here?" she asked.

Seeing the astonished looks on the selectmen's faces, she said, "All possibilities must be examined."

Keith was adamant in his quick response.

"No."

Keith polled the selectboard with a look.

"We don't. We think Gaige is off the reservation."

"Gaige?" Idalene asked mildly.

"Gaige LaRoche. Don't know if you remember. It was a number of years ago, but Gaige led a demonstration against a housing development. He said the clam flats near the site would be destroyed. The suspicion is he is the one that eventually contaminated the clam flats to prove his point. The guy is a real weirdo. Went to school for biology or something scientific and can't get a job in his profession."

Idalene was elated. Her plan was falling into place so nicely.

"Well then, I guess a special permit may be in

order. We will certainly look at that."

"Look at these fools grin. You would think it was Christmas." Idalene thought.

"To show his support for this emergency situation, the governor would like to hold a special joint press conference here in West Bath tonight. He would like all of you to be present. Is there a good site for this news conference? In addition, he would also like to hold a public meeting to answer questions here in the next few days. Is that something you can organize?"

"Frank, make the public information session happen. Get the fire station. A press conference tonight may be more difficult. We are too small here at the town office. The fire station is out of the question. It's too public. The school doesn't have enough notice." Keith said.

Frank said, "We could hold it at the [25]Grange."

---

25   **Grange**: 1860's Patrons of Husbandry Union of Farmers. Commonly referred to as "The Grange" in Maine. A number of towns in Maine still proudly have an active Grange.

Chapter 23

Idalene rocketed back to Augusta to tie up the loose ends of her plan. She was delighted as she walked into her office, with Polly at her heels.

Sitting at her desk, Idalene extended her well manicured hand for the newspapers that Polly held out to her. The headlines were perfect. She held up one for Polly to read.

"Governor's office denies bad clam connection to deaths in West Bath."

She flipped up another one.

"Is West Bath covering up clam contamination?"

Polly, of course, had actually read the articles and was aghast at Idalene's callousness.

"This is exactly what we need. Now we need to tie in LaRoche." Idalene grinned. "Polly, start slowly spreading rumors in the online network about LaRoche being an eco-terrorist. Make sure you remind the news outlets of his involvement in that clam flats incident in North Bath. That should keep the media going for a while and give us time to kill that moose."

She dropped the newspapers on the desk.

"Has the Portland paper come in yet?"

Polly handed her a stack of online news reports, along with printouts from several blogs. Idalene scanned them all and laughed.

"Excellent. Let's keep the focus there."

She handed the reports back to Polly.

"Draft up a press release from the governor that will help the news outlets to make a connection to LaRoche," Polly worked hard to keep her face neutral. Idalene's eyes narrowed almost imperceptibly.

"On second thought," Idalene said, "perhaps I should handle this myself. Just to make sure it gets done correctly. Why don't you start drafting a speech for the governor, announcing a special moose hunt to handle the overpopulation of moose in West Bath and hinting that someone has somehow manufactured another eco-scare? You should be able to handle that."

Polly could still hear Idalene laughing as she sat down at her desk. It hadn't taken long for this last insult from Idalene to push Polly to the edge. She walked out of the building and across the parking lot. Scanning the area for eavesdroppers, she took her tablet out of her purse and verified the information.

Looking over her shoulder again, she took out her cell phone and called her cousin, who just happened to be the governor of [26]New Hampshire.

"Abby, this is Polly."

"Polly, how are you doing? I haven't talked to you since the last reunion. How are the kids?"

"Really good. We should get together and catch up. Abby, have you heard about the moose attacks in West Bath?" Polly asked.

"Yes, I have. Is it really a moose?"

"Looks that way. I have some information you might be interested in about this. There's significant spin going on here. I'm going to send this stuff to you." Polly highlighted some of the more egregious misstatements being issued by the Maine governor's office through Idalene.

"I can't believe she is telling these lies when people have died. It's like the citizens don't matter to her," Polly said.

Abby Pickering listened silently, taking notes. "Well, that is interesting news. Yes, send it to my personal email and copy it to my aide. Thanks for calling, Polly. We do need to get together soon. Maybe a shopping trip to Boston is in order. In fact, we could make a family day of it and bring the kids. I bet they would love seeing the aquarium and shopping at [27]Quincy Market."

26   Maine has the distinction of having a boarder with only one other state – New Hampshire.

27   **Quincy Market, North Market, Faneuil Hall and South Market**: History-rich section of Boston that served as a platform

Zombie Moose

Governor Pickering drummed her hands on her desk before buzzing her aide.

"You should be getting an email from my cousin, Polly, in a few minutes. There should be several documents and an audio file. We need to get moving on those right away. You'll understand when you read them. It looks like it's a killer moose and that moron of a governor in Maine is allowing his chief of staff to orchestrate a cover-up. See what you can verify independently. We're going to blow them out of the water. Go ahead and schedule a news conference in time to make the evening news. Invite the national guys as well."

Governor Pickering watched the door close before chuckling. "[28]The way life should be, indeed."

---

for the firebrands that lead the American Revolution. Today it is an awesome shopping site.

28   **State Motto**: "The way life should be" would be a really cool state motto. It is unofficially second only to "Vacation land." Unfortunately, some nimrod back in the day thought that "Dirigo" would be a show stopper of a motto and, embarrassingly, the state legislature agreed.

Chapter 24

"I don't want to go home. Satan is still out there," Lottie protested.

"Ma, it's a moose and you can't stay in the hospital."

"I ain't going home."

"Ma, you're being silly."

"Mayhap so, son, but I ain't going back."

Larry sighed and plopped in the chair, snatching up the channel changer.

"Ma, they're going to discharge you today and you'll have to leave."

"Nope."

Larry scowled as he flipped through various television channels. He caught sight of his sedated mother on one of the news stations, even though the reporters were prevented access to her by the paramedics. Lottie's attention was also focused on the television. She blanched at the pictures of Scott's body being loaded into the ambulance.

"Son, I can't go back there."

Horrified, Larry watched as reporters clamored for interviews, nodded his head in agreement, but for an entirely different reason.

"Why don't I get you a room at one of the hotels? That way you won't be bothered with reporters. We'll check you in under a false name."

Lottie continued to watch, shuddering as the reporter described the attack.

"I guess that would be for the best."

Satisfied, Larry handed Lottie the channel changer.

"Good. I'll go make the arrangements."

Lottie clicked off the television and threw her head back onto the pillow. Tears seeped from the corners of her eyes as she squeezed them shut.

"It's coming for us all! Evil is walking the earth! We must run!"

There was a discreet knock on the door.

"Lottie, are you awake?"

Myrna Jessup, Lottie's cousin, came in. They had spent a great deal of time together as children, and Myrna considered Lottie to be more of a really weird sister than a cousin. Instead of rejecting Lottie's eccentricities, Myrna embraced them. As they aged, Lottie became rounder, and Myrna became stately. With her long gray hair flowing behind her, Myrna swept into Lottie's hospital room.

"There you are. Lands, you are white as a ghost. I know you've witnessed something horrible. I sense that your spirit is still troubled."

"Oh, Myrna, you should have seen the hell spawn! It may look like a moose, but it's a demon with fur."

Myrna patted Lottie's hand.

"It's okay, Lottie. That's why I'm here. I just thought you might need some answers to what you saw, as well as some spiritual guidance. See, I have my [29]Tarot deck. We'll just see what the cards have to tell us."

Myrna held up the brightly colored deck.

"Myrna, you know I don't put any stock in those mumbo-jumbo things."

Myrna smiled.

"Well, it's not going to hurt to just do one reading. And you don't have to act on what the cards say if you don't want to. It's just to help you sort things out."

Lottie frowned at the cards.

"I guess it can't hurt. What do I do?"

Myrna patted Lottie's hand again. Sweeping off the tableside tray, she adopted a softer tone.

"Just clear your mind and form a question. You don't even have to tell me what it is. Just clear your

---

29   **Tarot**: Originally a card game. Still haven't quite figured out how it made the leap to divination.

mind and relax."

Lottie lay back on her pillows.

"It's hard to get that evil beast out of my mind."

"Well, let's ask a question about the moose then."

"It's Satan," Lottie insisted.

"Well, maybe, but let's focus on a particular question."

Lottie screwed up her face as she said, "Why didn't he kill me?"

Myrna held up a hand.

"The cards are for you. Can you rephrase the question?"

Lottie thought carefully.

"I reckon that I want to know why I was spared and that poor man wasn't."

Myrna nodded.

"Good. Let's see where the cards lead, shall we?"

Myrna fanned the deck in her hands.

"Select the card that will be your significator."

Lottie looked at the fanned cards.

"That's bigger than a regular deck of cards. I don't know which one to pick."

Myrna smiled gently.

"Leave that to fate. Just pick a random card."

Lottie closed her eyes tight. Her hand hovered over first one card, then another, before slowly pulling one from the deck.

"Excellent."

Myrna took the card and placed it on the bedside

table then shuffled the deck.

"Ah. The High Priestess."

Lottie sat up to get a better look at the card.

"Well, what does it mean?"

"This is the card that signifies you. Is there a reason why you shouldn't remain neutral? Is there something that you should be acting on?"

"Well, there are my whoopie pies. I need to get those in the freezer."

Myrna chuckled.

"No. As it pertains to your question. The High Priestess symbolizes the unknown future or secrets and mystery."

"Well, it is a mystery why I wasn't killed."

Myrna pulled the next card off the top of the deck.

"Let's see what the card signifying the past says."

Lottie gasped as Myrna turned over Death.

Myrna held up her hand.

"Death is not necessarily a bad thing. It signifies change and it is reversed. Have you usually taken a path of inactivity in the past?"

Lottie's eyes widened.

"Yes. [30]I don't like messing in other folk's troubles."

---

30 Lottie was the snoopiest neighbor down at Birch Point and seemed to have an internal radar for other folks' troubles. If something was going on, she would ferret it out.

Myrna nodded.

"The next card signifies growth."

Myrna turned the next card.

"Ah, Ten of Swords reversed. This signifies power and authority."

"Oh my," Lottie whispered.

Myrna flipped over the fourth card.

"Knight of Swords. Bravery, war, wrath. Is there a battle you need to fight?"

Lottie became very still.

Myrna revealed the fifth card.

"Ten of Wands reversed. Are you entering a situation where there will be difficulties and intrigues?"

Lottie reached for a card and turned it over and gasped again.

"The Devil. This is a card of ravage, force and what is predestined," Myrna said.

Lottie's hands clamped onto Myrna's arm.

"I know why I was spared. I was allowed to see this evil with my own eyes and was saved to fight it. I have been called!"

Myrna's mouth opened, but she couldn't form any words. She looked down at the card tableau and reached out, and placed her hand on Lottie's arm.

"Now, Lottie, these are just to help you organize your thoughts, find some focus. There may be another interpretation. We need to look at all the cards in context."

"And it has, Myrna, don't you see! You were sent

to me to open my eyes. I have been called! Just like that Knight of Swords!"

Lottie snatched the deck from a very surprised Myrna.

"Does it matter how many I lay out?"

Lottie collected the cards from the tableau and shuffled the deck.

Myrna was stunned.

"I don't think so," she said hesitantly.

"So one card is all I need?"

"It's more important to clear your mind and center your thoughts, Lottie."

Lottie pulled a card from the center of the deck.

"Will someone who is close to me die?"

She

had flipped over the card. It was Death.

Suddenly buzzers sounded and bells rang. The hospital intercom began to blare out a Code Blue.

The two women craned their necks to watch people running into the room across the hall. Lottie went white. Looking up at Myrna she said, "Oh, my!"

She quickly shuffled the deck again and pulled another card.

"Will I be free to follow my destiny?" Lottie asked in a quavering voice. Myrna leaned forward. Lottie slowly turned over the card. Justice.

Myrna grabbed for the deck.

"Lottie, that's not how these work!"

Lottie held them out of reach.

"Give those back to me!" Myrna demanded.

In the ensuing tussle, the deck was scattered all over the room. Lottie had a fist full of Myrna's hair to prevent her from retrieving any more of the cards. A couple of nurses ran into the room and separated the two old women.

Myrna was escorted from the building by two strapping security guards.

"That's not how it works, you idiot," Myrna was screaming as they led her away.

"Keep the stupid deck, you old bat. I can just get another one. A better one."

Lottie was smiling.

"Justice," she said to the nurse who was checking her vitals.

Chapter 25

Gaige placed the samples in sterile containers and returned them to the refrigerator.

"I need a better lab," he said.

Slumping down in a chair, he put his head in his hands. His brow knit into ridges and his eyes closed as he ran through various possibilities. The options narrowed as he rejected each one before exploring the next. Suddenly, his eyes popped opened and his mouth relaxed.

"Of course! He owes me a favor!"

Snatching up the phone, he quickly punched in a number.

"Yes, can I have the lab, please? I'm looking for Egan Tyler. This is Gaige LaRoche."

Gaige impatiently waited for the call to transfer to the lab then told the woman who answered that he was looking for Egan Tyler.

Egan was a classmate of Gaige's in college, not

a friend. Like the majority of the student body, Egan had been infected with Professor Johnson's dislike of Gaige and had very little to do with him. Egan wasn't particularly brilliant, however he was a steady student and had solid prospects to look forward to.

It was late spring just before graduation when Egan had mistakenly put the wrong beaker on the burner. The titanium tetrachloride ignited, sending poisonous gas throughout the science wing. Gaige had saved Egan from scandal by taking the blame. Gaige knew Egan was about to be married and had some job interviews lined up after graduation. Egan had a lot on his mind and Gaige felt sorry for him. It had been an honest mistake. Gaige had known Johnson would find some way to blame it on him anyway.

Egan had felt so grateful about his escape from public disgrace that he had invited Gaige to his wedding. One thing led to another, including some reception photos of Gaige and Egan downing beers and Egan stripping down to his shorts and dancing using the beer kegs as props. Unfortunately these photos ended up on the Internet.

During Egan's job interviews discussion concerning those pictures came up more often than not.

The upshot was that Egan's new bride forbid him to have any contact with Gaige again. Ever. As time passed, Egan had convinced himself it was actually Gaige who set the titanium tetrachloride on fire.

Because of their history, Gaige thought Egan would come through for him now.

"Tyler here. How can I help you?"

"Egan, this is Gaige. How you doing?"

The phone disconnected immediately.

"Well, that was weird."

Hitting redial, Gaige reconnected with the hospital operator.

"I was disconnected. This is Gaige LaRoche. Could you please reconnect me with Egan Tyler in the lab again?"

"Oh, I'm sorry, sir. Just a moment."

When Egan answered again, Gaige said, "Egan, I desperately need your help."

Egan hissed into the phone, "Gaige, whatever it is, the answer is no."

Gaige bit his lip.

"You're not still mad about that incident at your reception, are you?"

"Are you kidding? You nearly ruined my wedding night. It was almost the first ever wedding that ended with divorce after six hours."

Egan scanned the lab to see if anyone was listening.

"I'm not even going to talk about the time you nearly killed me in college. Every time I get anywhere near you something goes horribly wrong or blows up. It was months before my eyebrows grew back after you set the lab on fire."

Gaige took a deep breath.

"You know that —"

"Know what? Huh? You said you did it. Live with it," Egan snapped.

Gaige grimaced.

"Look, I just need you to run something through your lab. It's important," Gaige said.

"No."

"It's about that moose that's been killing people."

Egan shouted, "Oh. My. Lands. Stay away from me. Don't call again. I might lose my job just talking to you. I'm married, with kids. Go away."

He slammed down the phone as his co-workers stopped what they were doing to stare at him.

Egan's supervisor walked toward him.

Egan picked up the phone and dialed the hospital operator.

"Whatever you do, if Gaige LaRoche calls back, or anyone sounding like Gaige LaRoche, do not put them through."

"Egan, are you okay? Why are you so upset?" the lab supervisor asked.

Egan sighed deeply.

"Yes. I'm fine."

He smiled and waved his hand at the rest of the lab staff.

"I need to take a short break if that's okay with you."

The lab supervisor nodded.

"Take all the time you need."

Egan went outside and sat at one of the picnic tables. He drummed his fingers on the tabletop for a few moments before pulling a business card from his wallet.

Punching in a number he said, "Yes, how much does a restraining order cost?"

Gaige called the lab again. The hospital operator's voice once again asked how she could help him.

"Please connect me with the lab."

"May I get your name?"

"Gaige LaRoche."

"I am sorry, Mr. LaRoche, Mr. Tyler has asked that we block your calls. Can I take a message?"

Gaige hung up without responding and, as he did before he had attempted to make that useless call, he slumped back into his chair.

Chapter 26

Quinn went back to work, promising to bring Gaige some dinner before she went home. She had stopped by the post office to pick up the company mail and grabbed the newspaper on her way in. When she opened the paper, there was a story that hinted Gaige had created this "ecological emergency" to get attention for another one of his environmental causes. It didn't say anything about the moose. Instead, the story focused on when Gaige was in high school.

It was the story of his failed attempt to save the clam flat. There was even a current quote from one of the residents at the development stating he was glad the site had been developed and that the clams had never been missed.

Quinn sat at her computer and pulled up several blogs that had been written in response to the article. They all said pretty much the same thing. Some of the more extreme commentary actually speculated that

Gaige had been doing gene manipulation on clams that, if eaten, resulted in people's heads exploding.

"I can't believe this! What were they doing? They are completely ignoring what is happening," thought Quinn. "Gaige is the only one who's actually trying to solve this, and they're making him look like a crazy person."

Quinn shoved her chair back from the desk.

"That does it. I'm moving him in with me. Someone has got to protect him."

Pushing the newspaper into the trash, she grabbed her keys and headed for Gaige's apartment.

She snatched Gaige's newspaper from his front door step and dropped it over the railing. Once inside, she found him bowed over his notes. He looked up at her through bleary eyes.

"Oh, is it dinner time already?"

Quinn pursed her lips.

"Lost track of time, did you?"

She looked around at the messy kitchen.

"I need better equipment," he whined.

"I know. You also need a place to stay. How much of this stuff would you have to take with you?"

"What?" He looked around. "My clothes and lab equipment is all. The place came furnished."

"Well, that's easy. Do you have any boxes? Let's go. You're going to stay with me until you find a new place."

"I need a place to set up my lab."

"I have a laundry room that will work just fine."

Gaige stood up and looked around. Quinn watched the confusion cross his face. He does take some looking after, she thought. "You go take care of your lab stuff. I'll grab your clothes."

***

Moving Gaige had not been as difficult as Quinn had anticipated. They were able to pack everything he owned into their two cars. Upon arriving at her house, Gaige immediately disappeared into Quinn's laundry room with his lab equipment.

Meanwhile, Quinn did not stay idle either. When she left to go pick up pizza, she also purchased some burner phones. She gave one to Gaige and took his cell phone, explaining it would allow him to work without interruption. With Gaige working in her house, she could shield him from the lies floating around.

The bonus was, she had access to his research and was able to get several photographs of the tests he was performing. With a few simple questions, Gaige was able to supply enough evidence to effectively counter the misinformation about him with hard facts.

***

Idalene was all smiles around the office. She had checked various sites and was nearly chortling with joy. She would be meeting with the senatorial candidate soon about working for him. Life was good.

Maybe the candidate would like to see some of the work I've done to spin this potential crisis.

She was perusing several news sites when an alert popped up for Sea Smoke.

Idalene glared at the computer screen. There were several pictures of microscope slides and scribbled notes on the blog site. Idalene stabbed the intercom button.

"Polly, get in here!" she barked, "Now!"

Polly jumped when Idalene's voice exploded through the intercom. Her eyes darted around at the nearby desks as her throat tightened. Trying to calm herself, she stood and gathered a note pad before walking the short distance to Idalene's office.

Polly swallowed and took a deep breath before opening the door.

"Where are you on this Sea Smoke thing?"

Idalene waved a hand at her computer.

Polly felt her shoulders relax.

"Oh, the blogger. That is a tough one. He's covered his tracks pretty well."

Idalene slammed her hand down on the desk.

"You need to uncover them."

Polly backed up a step.

"I thought you didn't think one blogger was that important."

Idalene's eyes flashed as she studied Polly's face.

"I don't pay you to think."

"Yes, ma'am. I'll get right on that."

Not waiting for a dismissal, Polly turned and fled. When she returned to her desk, she looked quickly around to ensure she was not being observed, and forwarded Sea Smoke's link to her cousin in New Hampshire.

Chapter 27

Disappointed, Gaige considered Quinn's laundry room to be barely more adequate as a lab than his apartment kitchen had been. He called another old acquaintance from college.

"Sandy, it's Gaige. I need some help. There's something going on that isn't right."

"Gaige? Last time I tried to help you out I almost got expelled. You have the luck of Hiram Smith. Stay away."

Sandy hung up.

Gaige glared at the phone and called her again.

"Go away, Gaige," Sandy warned.

Gaige shouted over her into the phone. "Sandy, don't hang up! A moose is killing people and may be eating them."

"Sandy? Sandy, you there?"

Silence greeted him.

"Sandy?" Gaige pulled the phone away from his

ear and frowned at it. It appeared to still be connected.

"Sandy? You there?"

"I'm here," Sandy mumbled.

"Listen, I've seen the moose. It was six inches from me and, I don't know why, but it didn't attack. There is a sour stink about it that I haven't been able to isolate. From the tests on my samples, I'm convinced that it is an organic issue and can be resolved. I'm concerned it may be transmittable to the rest of the moose population. I have samples, but I need a better research facility to ascertain what the cause is. The cops have the information from the three attack sites all locked up," Gaige paused.

"Sandy, you there?"

Sandy was already pulling up the information on her computer. Gaige may be a lightning rod for trouble, but this could be a gold mine. She grabbed her mouse.

"How did I miss this one?" she thought.

He waited for the response that didn't come.

"Just check it out and call me back. We need to get a crew together and find out what's going on. I would like to send you what I've found out. Can I send this data to you?"

Sandy's wide eyes didn't move from the computer screen. Keeping her voice disinterested she said, "Okay. I'll look at your data." She supplied him with her email address.

"Thank you." Gaige supplied the number for the burner phone. "Think about it and call me back."

Sandy had hit the disconnect button on the phone. Her eyes grew rounder as she pulled up information on the moose attacks. Her hand fumbled its way back to the phone. Stealing a quick look at the keypad, she punched in a number.

Not waiting for introductions, as soon as her call was answered, she said, "Have you seen these reports about a moose killing people? It looks like it was buried in the news, but there are some reports from yesterday still floating around."

She waited for the response.

"No. Gaige LaRoche called me. He said he's seen the moose and he thinks," Sandy shook her head. "I know he's a screw-up and I'm not thrilled he is the one who brought this to my attention. However, it is compelling. Yes, it would make an excellent piece of research. It is too bad we have to deal with Gaige. The problem is that he has all the samples and Johnson will never let him back in his lab." She frowned.

"I'm not excited about sharing a byline with him. However, I might be able to get around that little issue."

Meanwhile, Gaige had no confidence that Sandy would help him. He hadn't had any contact with her since college. She was a freshman when he graduated. She had been one of his few friends until Egan's titanium tetrachloride incident.

At first she had defended him, but ended up as distant as everyone else at school was. While she didn't buy into Johnson's opinion that Gaige was a showboat using science to gain media attention, she now believed him to be a sloppy scientist, careless in his approach.

Sandy was a long shot at best. Gaige let his head drop to his chest. He wished he could order a lab up from Acme like that cartoon character did. It never worked out too well for the coyote either, he thought. Straightening his shoulders, he walked back to his makeshift lab. He picked up the computer printouts and studied them.

The more he discovered, the more convinced he became. Dropping the printouts he thought, "This information will speak for itself. I just need to get someone with a lab to listen."

Gaige stared unseeing at his notes piled on top of the washing machine.

"Even with this sorry bunch of data, the evidence is compelling. Come on Gaige, think! Where can you find a lab?"

He walked into the living room and stopped in front of a picture of Quinn's grandmother standing next to Senator Susan Collins. He reached out and touched the frame.

"Well, it's a shot," he said.

Walking back into the laundry, he moved to his laptop on the ironing board and looked up a contact point for the state government. He had to make a number of calls and endure numerous re-routings before someone besides a receptionist or secretary actually took his call.

When he finally reached a decision maker, it was the assistant director in the Maine Department of Tourism.

Chapter 28

While Gaige was downstairs making phone calls, Quinn was in the attic reviewing news reports. She noted the sameness that was embedded in most of the stories surrounding the moose attacks. Moving to another article that completely ignored the moose and focused on bad clams, she realized she was beginning to see the thread regarding eco-terrorism as a prominent theme.

Quinn's Nana had always said, "Just because your cat had kittens in the oven don't make them biscuits. Just because folks are saying this doesn't mean it's based on facts." Quinn leaned back in her chair and ran her hand through her hair. Someone is definitely spoon-feeding the media. I need to get some facts and find out who is running this show.

She frowned at the clock as she picked up her phone. She listened to it ring a few times on the other end before it was answered.

"So, you must be by yourself if you're answering the phone," she said. "Yes, I did know it's getting late. I'm just glad I caught you. I need you to do something for me. Can I run by the office right now?"

Quinn's smile widened.

"How often do I ask you for stuff? This will be all kinds of fun. I promise!"

Her eye's twinkled at the response.

"I'll be right there."

Quinn opened the door to the old two-story office and navigated her way up the narrow staircase.

"Hello? Dean? You still here?"

The smell of old books and dust warmed by the sun surrounded her. Quinn moved her way past the reception area to the office.

"What? No balloons? I thought you said this would be fun!" Dean Crane said.

Dean had been Quinn's grandmother's personal attorney and close friend for years. Quinn saw no reason to end the relationship after her grandmother had passed. The law firm Dean was a partner in chose to maintain the facade of this little office as a sole proprietor to be close to their most important and eccentric client. Day to day, Dean handled estate planning, business issues, a few minor criminal cases, and all legal matters for Quinn's little fuel oil company. The real reason his firm maintained this fiction was to be readily available to this family to help manage their extensive holdings.

"It will be. You are going to love doing this."

She gave him a hug.

"It's all spy stuff."

Dean raised his eyebrow, "Oh?"

She passed him the thumb drive.

"Take a look and see what you think."

He took the thumb drive and plugged it into his computer. Quinn plopped down in the chair and started flipping through a sailing magazine.

"Okay. What do you want me to do?" he finally said.

"What do you think?"

Dean nodded.

"I think your scientist friend is on to something. I also think someone wants to discredit him and draw attention away from the moose issue."

"It's what I think, too. I need to find out who's behind this."

Quinn smiled, "I was hoping you could make those inquiries for me so it can't be traced back to me."

Dean turned his chair to the window overlooking the City of Bath. He liked it here. It provided him with a relaxed environment and, because of Quinn, it kept his bank account where he wanted it. Besides, he liked doing spy stuff.

Turning back to Quinn, he said, "How soon do you need the information?"

"Pretty quickly, before much more damage can be done," Quinn said. "I'd like to have something in the next day or two."

Dean pursed his lips. He liked the challenge, but the lawyer in him kept him from showing his delight.

"I'll give you a call tomorrow."

He reached into his drawer and pulled out a file.

"In the meantime, I'll return the favor. I was going to call you to come in for a visit. I want you to take a look at something as well."

Puzzled, Quinn took the folder.

"I'm not that young whipper-snapper your grandmother knew anymore. The firm thinks that maybe it's time to take on a partner at my little office."

Quinn shook her head.

"I haven't asked for that."

Dean held up his hand.

"I know. I do appreciate your confidence. However, I'll be sixty-seven on my next birthday. I should be out sailing more."

Quinn looked out the window toward the river.

"Yes, you should," Quinn said.

She thumped the file.

"I'll take a look. I doubt I'll find anyone to replace you."

"You can start interviewing for my partner when you're ready," Dean said. "If you don't like the ones in the file, we can give you some more. However, we think you will find these candidates acceptable. You have their complete bios there and comments from the senior partners,"

He smiled at her.

"I know you'll do your own checking. They've all been thoroughly screened. We had quite a few lining up for the position. We culled out the ones that wanted to use it as a career boost."

He reached out and patted Quinn's hand.

"I'll still be around. I like it here."

***

Quinn assigned Dean's file folder to her [31]Bean bag. There were more important things she needed to deal with. Now that she'd put Dean on the scent, she was ready to move to the next item on her agenda. She wanted to check out the area where Gaige has seen the moose. She negotiated the narrow streets leading out of the city and headed towards the woods of West Bath.

Even though there was plenty of daylight left, Quinn was not intending to actually go deep into the woods. In spite of what she was telling herself, the palms of her hands were sweaty on the steering wheel. It was easy to tell where Gaige had pulled off because of the tire tracks in the soft mud. She eased her car off the road.

---

31   **Bean Bag**: In 1911 Leon Leonwood (L.L. Bean) Bean created a boot that took the hunting world by storm. It wasn't long before his company (LL Bean, Inc.) became a famous source for excellent hunting and outdoor equipment. His boat bags (Bean Bags) are a big favorite of locals. They come in a variety of sizes and are so useful the design has been replicated just about everywhere.

Walking towards the tree line, Quinn checked her camera and started snapping off shots. Lowering the camera she walked a few feet into the woods and listened. Everything seemed normal. Recalling the pungent aroma surrounding Gaige this morning, she started sniffing for that same stench. Emboldened when she didn't detect anything to alarm her, she moved forward into the woods.

Despite the caution with which Quinn proceeded, she still jumped at every sound as she continued to search for that distinct scent. The darker and more inaccessible the woods became, the more she told herself she should turn around. However, she kept moving forward until she noted the absence of black flies and mosquitoes. Looking around carefully and sniffing, she located the offensive odor.

"Man, is that ripe!"

Staring hard in the direction the smell seemed to be coming from, she could see nothing. Clicking off several shots, she became more uncomfortable.

She said aloud, "Time to go, girl."

Quinn turned and ran back to her vehicle.

When she downloaded the pictures, she scanned through them. Leaning in, she sucked in a breath through her teeth. The pictures revealed that the moose was standing much closer to her than she knew.

"Yet, he didn't attack!" She thought.

Chapter 29

Idalene had been briefing the Governor on tonight's press conference. They would be leaving in a few moments. Polly had just sent a text that the cars were waiting. As she rounded the corner, she spotted Dave chatting it up with staff.

"I can't let the Governor see that idiot or he will want to take him to the conference," Idalene thought.

Walking on the far side of the room, she was able to avoid any contact with him. She did, however, commit to memory the faces of the slacking staffers surrounding Dave.

She was not able to avoid the group of grade school students touring the state capital.

"Children, there is Ms. Richie. She is like a special secretary to the Governor."

Idalene bristled, shooting a chilling smile to the teacher.

"Say hello to Ms. Richie."

The thin reedy voices of the children somehow managed to form the word, 'Hello.'

Idalene adjusted her smile.

"Why, hello children. What are you learning from your teacher today?"

Her tone caused staffers at the capital to turn and go in the other direction.

"That you're a secretary like my mom," one particularly sticky urchin piped.

Doors slammed shut in the background.

Idalene's smile tightened.

"Yes, just like your dear mother, I'm sure."

Staffers suddenly found they needed to talk with someone in another section of the building.

"Oh, no, baby," said a plump woman, "Ms. Richie isn't like me at all. She's Governor Pelletier's Chief of Staff."

The woman flashed a toothy smile.

"She does important work."

Idalene's teeth were grating. She managed to smile at the woman.

"I'm sure your work is just as important as what we do here, probably more so. You have a," Idalene paused, "very bright little boy. You should be proud."

The woman blushed happily and Idalene used the break in the conversation to avoid committing homicide.

"It was nice to meet all you wonderful children." She then had clear sailing. No one else was around to impede her progress.

Chapter 30

It was nearly 4:30 p.m., in the afternoon. Horace Penley, Assistant Director of Tourism for the State of Maine stopped working at 3:00 p.m. He told his staff he was using the "quiet time" to sort through his daily paperwork and didn't want to be disturbed. Technically, he was doing something with the paperwork. His head was lying on top of it, and he was drooling on it.

If the truth be known, Horace stopped working for the state after lunch-time when he returned to his desk. To look at him, as he pounded on the keyboard, he appeared to be getting a lot of work done. And he was working on his eBay business that involved selling black market festival memorabilia. For the most part, he kept his job with the state because he stayed out of the Tourism Director's way and never, ever showed up on anyone's radar.

Horace was startled from his nap when the intercom buzzed.

"Mr. Penley, Mr. LaRoche on line two."

Choking as he inhaled drool, he managed to cough out "I'm working here."

"I am sorry, sir, but Ms. Richie has asked that you take this call."

Horace was instantly wide awake and stared at the phone in a panic. He had no idea Idalene even knew who he was. He had stayed at the very back of the room during meetings. He didn't' make any waves, didn't put forward any ideas, and had successfully avoided appearing on camera.

Through years of practice, Horace knew how to school his voice to sound calm even in the most extreme circumstances.

"Did you find out what this is about?"

"Something about needing a laboratory in which to do experiments."

Horace's face froze.

"This must be a mistake. Does this person understand that we are the Department of Tourism?"

"Yes. Ms. Richie has asked that you take the call."

Horace tilted his head in thought.

"Is Idalene targeting me? Am i being set up for failure?"

His hand shook as he pressed the button for line two.

"Hello, this is Horace Penley. How can I help you?"

"Hi. Um, this is Gaige LaRoche. I may have some

information about the moose."

Horace's mind was racing.

"Moose? What moose?"

"The West Bath moose. The one that's killing people."

Relaxing, Horace leaned back in his chair.

"Oh. Right. I did hear something about that yesterday. I think the animal control guys are all over this. Old news already."

"I'm an animal control guy. I also know a little bit about animal biology. I think this moose is sick. We need to find out why, in case it's contagious."

"Oh, Mr. – LaRoche, is it? I don't think we need to be that alarmist. It's an isolated incident restricted to one small area. No need to worry."

Gaige slapped his head with his hand. "Mr. Penley —"

"Call me Horace. I know you might think there's some bigger conspiracy here. A lot of people seem to think the same thing. Really, there's no need for anyone to become excited about this. I barely remember hearing about the moose. I'm certain that our top men are working on the problem, and it will be over by tomorrow. Now those clams are a different story. I would warn you to stay away from clams for a while."

Nettled by Penley's off-handed dismissal of the danger, Gaige gritted his teeth.

"Mr. Penley, there aren't any bad clams. There is a large animal running around loose killing people. I've run some simple tests and have found some anomalies with the moose. I need to get access to a fully-equipped lab to isolate and identify those anomalies. I need to speak to the governor."

Penley sat up straight.

"Tests? Really? What kind of tests are we talking about?"

"On the animal's hair and mucus, and some local vegetation. Also, I noted that only one of the people killed was a native Mainer.

Horace was beginning to sweat.

"In fact, after the first kill, the moose ignored locals standing nearby and targeted only tourists. Don't you find that strange?"

Horace began to look wildly around his office for escape.

"Umm. Send me an email and I'll forward it to the governor. I want to warn you against blowing up something simple and creating a panic."

Penley was now up out of his chair and standing at his desk.

"Mr. LaRoche, let's not create a crisis where there is none. We will deal with the moose at the state level and the problem will be solved. Let me confer with the governor and get back to you."

Gaige groaned.

"Okay. Give me your email address. I'm sending this to you now. You will see that a better lab for me to work in is necessary. I've included my contact information. Please get back to me soon."

"I have to talk to Idalene," Horace thought.

Maintaining a calm voice, he thanked Gaige for his community mindedness before hanging up.

Gaige tossed the phone on the couch. I don't have time for this.

Chapter 31

Horace was sweating bullets. His whole career, he had managed to hide and be in the right place at the right time for promotions. Nothing greedy or ambitious. He carefully chose positions in state government that no one really wanted and had very little contact with the public. Tourism was an iffy choice, but it was either that or the Arts Council. Now he was faced with the most terrifying decision of his life. Idalene had sent the call to him. He knew she would expect a report.

Horace's finger had actually been on the intercom button to tell his secretary to call Idalene back with a report. He had been quite adept at hiding behind secretaries for decades. His survival senses told him he should do the deed. His lifelong pattern of blending into the background was screaming warnings. His hand hovered over the intercom button as he mustered up his resolve. Pressing the offending button down, he said, "Get Ms. Richie on the line for me."

The minutes stretched into years as he waited.

When the secretary rang him, he nearly had a heart attack. "Sir, Ms. Richie has left with the governor for a press conference in West Bath."

Horace leaned back in his chair. His relief was only momentary. Idalene had sent the call to him. If it had been anyone else, he would have just left a message. It wasn't anyone else. In all his years as a government lackey, he had never seen anyone as terrifying as this young blonde woman. He just knew it was a test of some sort; she was singling him out of the herd for slaughter. To complicate matters, the email from LaRoche had just landed in his inbox.

With his stomach in a knot, he said, "Please get Ms. Richie on her cell."

Idalene was grinning.

"Yes, Horace, we are tracking all information on the moose. Calm down and start at the beginning. No, tourism will not be ruined. You don't say. Scientific research? Why, yes, please send Polly any information —" Idalene paused, "Yes, Mr. LaRoche may have stumbled on to something. Thank you for this heads up."

"Yes, indeed, Mr. LaRoche, you will make a fine distraction. We have your research now and the log of your many calls to the state house. You've done the heavy lifting to paint yourself as a nut job. With your history, your current apocalyptic ramblings will go through the press like [32]salts through a goose."

Idalene looked at Polly in the seat beside her.

"When we arrive in West Bath, let me know as soon as the email from Horace arrives. We may need to leak it right away, so get that set up now. Make certain LaRoche's failed clam flat protests and his inability to get a job in his profession gets leaked with it."

Smiling, she returned to reviewing the talking points for the governor's press conference as the caravan continued down the road to West Bath.

---

32   **Like salts through a goose**: without getting into the lurid details, they mean something that happens wicked fast.

Chapter 32

Sandy spent several hours going over the information Gaige had forwarded to her. Now she sat twirling her ink pen in her fingers, not focusing.

The data was good. The moose could possibly be cured. This was a wicked gold mine. She had been looking for a research subject and this gem fell right into her lap. Too bad she needed Gaige's samples or she would cut him out completely.

Her hands grew still and she laid down her pen. Her eyes refocused.

"Of course, this would work. With his reputation, no one would believe him if he ever claimed the data was his. Now who can I get for interns on this project?"

She flipped through some notes and smiled.

"This is going to work."

Sandy was able to enlist the help of Professor Zoe L'Heureux in exchange for an exclusive on the moose story.

Zombie Moose

L'Heureux taught Renaissance literature, but she made her real money from writing lurid true crime stories under the pen name of Margo Kapler. Sandy was one of the few people who knew about L'Heureux's sideline. Of course, everyone knew Professor Johnson was crazy about L'Heureux and that she had been fighting him off for years. For Sandy's purposes, this was going to be a win-win. She made herself a cup of tea and dialed Gaige's number.

Gaige was opening his second can of Moxie[33] when Sandy called. He had just finished talking with Penley at the Department of Tourism and did not have high hopes of getting a lab. He snatched up the phone immediately.

"Sandy, believe me, the data is good," he blurted out.

"I know it is, Gaige," Sandy said.

Gaige's eyebrows went up and his eyes widened.

"You do? Of course, you do. The numbers don't lie. All I need is a good lab to confirm the data. I think I may be able to cure the moose," Gaige blurted out.

"I think curing the moose is possible as well if the weird organic matter can be identified. I believe I can help you out. Can we meet someplace this evening?

33   **Moxie:** Patent medicine created in 1876 that became a popular soda. It is still fairly popular in Maine and even has its own festival every year in Lisbon Falls, Maine. There is no middle ground with this soda. You either really like it or you think it's just flat nasty and foist it on people from away just for fun.

I'll fill you in on the plan I have to get you into the lab here."

"Has Johnson agreed to allow me in there?"

"No. But I don't think that will be any kind of an issue," Sandy said. "Bring your samples with you and we'll get them cooking tonight."

"Really? Tonight? No problem. Thanks so much. I really owe you for this one." Gaige gushed.

Sandy picked up her pen and began to twirl it in her fingers.

"We can discuss a return of favors later. Let's get this moose cured first."

Chapter 33

It wasn't that Governor Pelletier hated press conferences. They were, after all, part and parcel of being a politician. It was all about name recognition and the best way to get name recognition is to have the press's attention. He understood that giving them something to write about would get his name in the news.

It was just that Governor Pelletier never really knew what to say. He had a sincere appreciation for Dave, who seemed to know exactly what to say in every situation. Governor Pelletier always felt a little awkward standing in front of a bunch of reporters, and was grateful for Idalene, who did such a great job prepping him.

Now, making speeches to supporters was something different. He loved doing that. He could just feel the goodwill washing over him when he gave those talks. It really didn't matter so much what you said as long as you said it with feeling. Governor Pelletier eyed the growing group of bored reporters gathering in the auditorium of the West Bath Grange and sighed.

Idalene had briefed him before they left the capital, and after they arrived at the Grange. She had given him a few minutes to gather himself while she hurried off to make certain everything was in place. Idalene made him nervous. She was meticulous and efficient, perfect traits for a chief of staff. He looked around the room and spotted her baring her teeth at some reporter she was talking to. It reminded him of the children's poem about the smiling crocodile.

He studied his notes still unable to make the connection between the moose and bad clams. Idalene had told him what to say. It had made sense when she explained it to him, but now it was no longer so clear. He really wished Dave was here. Idalene had gone to the front of the room and was announcing him. Showtime. He plastered on his best smile and went to work.

***

Harriet was on her way to midweek worship services and passed by the Grange. She hadn't had time to eat after volunteering at the food pantry in Bath. She noticed the cars in the Grange parking lot.

"Oh, there must be a [34]bean supper!"

---

34   **Bean suppers**: Community dinners. Not necessarily including beans. Usually connected with fund raisers.

She glanced at her watch and nodded.

"I have a few minutes, I'll just run in and grab a plate to go."

She turned into the parking lot and was pleased to find a spot open. Grabbing her wallet, she checked to make certain she had some cash.

"Ms. I need to check your —"

Harriet stopped with her opened her wallet. "How much do the tickets cost?" she asked in a low growl.

"Oh, um," The man checking credentials at the door took one look at Harriet and decided to let her pass unchallenged into the press conference.

"You can just go right in."

"Is the cashier inside?" Harriet asked, surprised. The credential checker was confused.

"Um."

Harriet peered up at the young man.

He quickly moved out of her way,

"Go right in, ma'am."

"Well, thank you."

Harriet was even more pleased. Maybe it's a benefit for someone. I can donate inside.

Beyond the Grange door, the press conference had been going on for several minutes.

"Governor, are you saying there is no killer moose?"

"There have been no confirmed reports of a rampaging moose. When," the Governor glanced at

Idalene and chuckled, "and if, we do get hard facts, we will act on them."

"But Governor, there's pictures on the internet of a moose killing people."

The governor looked pensive. "Ah, the internet. We also have pictures of Big Foot and Nessie on the internet. What we need to do is make sure there are —"

It was at that moment that Harriet threw the doors open at the back of the auditorium and marched in.

Everyone's attention was drawn to the back of the room. The governor blanched. "Well, uh, you see, it's, um —"

His head swiveled as he looked for Idalene.

The press was immediately alerted to the potential for a real story and began to pay close attention to what the governor was doing.

Unable to locate Idalene, the governor's eyes locked on Harriet. She looked like his Great Aunt Flossie who used to rap his knuckles with a wooden spoon whenever he opened his mouth. Aunt Flossie had always seemed to know when he was lying and what it was he was trying to hide from her. This woman standing at the back of the room had those same piercing eyes. The governor shifted his focus to Harriet's large handbag and wondered if it contained a wooden spoon.

The beads of sweat forming on the governor's face did not escape the notice of the reporters.

Their collected heads spun as one as they shifted to look at the object of the governor's attention.

Embarrassed, Harriet exclaimed, "Excuse me! This is wrong."

With the rumble of her voice still echoing in the Grange hall, she exited.

"Well, it's a matter of, uh, —"

The governor stepped away from the podium. His head was swimming with memories of time spent with his vicious Aunt.

"I need to go."

Panicked, he turned and ran through the nearest door.

The reporters were in a frenzy to get an interview or photograph of the mysterious woman and didn't notice the governor's escape. Chairs were overturned as reporters tried to disentangle themselves in time to be the first to interview Harriet. When the throng pushed their way past the door and reached the parking lot, she was already driving away. Stunned, they watched as her tail lights disappeared into the twilight. Undaunted, the pack turned as a group and converged on the overwhelmed credential checker.

Except for Idalene, the governor's staff was in a state of confusion. The governor had ducked into a closet and wouldn't come out until "the woman" was gone.

Idalene turned to Polly and hissed, "Find out who that woman is and what she knows. Now."

Idalene wasn't overly worried. Her plan was still in place. The reporters had something fresh to report that wasn't directly related to the moose. She just needed to get the background on this new wrinkle so she would be able to maintain control.

What Harriet had been thinking as she stood at the back of the building was, "This isn't a bean supper. I wonder if I still have time to grab a lobster roll at [35]Fat Boys before church services tonight."

---

35   **Fat Boys**: Popular drive-in located in Brunswick, Maine. Serves as a local harbinger of spring.

Chapter 34

Gaige wasted no time in collecting some samples after Sandy's call. Before he ran out the door, he scrawled a note on one of his research folders and stuffed it in the bottom of Quinn's Bean bag.

When he arrived at the coffee shop, he fretted about leaving the samples in the car and decided to take them with him. He scanned the interior, but didn't see her. Tightening his grip on the cooler, Gaige moved to the counter to order his coffee.

The young man behind the counter watched Gaige's approach, his eyes flickering to the red and white cooler Gaige was carrying. Gaige's eye's went to the overwhelming coffee menu and then to the young man's name tag.

"Jerry, do you have any Moxie?" Gaige asked.

Jerry sneered.

"No. We have some flavored sparkling water though."

Jerry's gaze returned to the cooler. Gaige lifted the cooler and put it up on the counter. He looked at the display of sparkling water.

"Any just plain old water?"

The word "samples" was scrawled across the front of the old cooler.

Jerry stepped back.

"Hey, don't set that there," Jerry sniped. "What's in it?"

"My stuff," Gaige snapped.

"Well, get your stuff off the counter," Jerry responded.

The testosterone escalated to dangerous levels as the door opened and Sandy arrived.

Gaige jerked the cooler off the counter and scowled at Jerry.

"Right."

"You going to order anything?" Jerry said. "When you have something people can actually drink, I will."

"What are you, blind?"

Jerry pointed to the menu board.

Gaige looked up at the menu board again.

"I'll get back to you on that, okay?"

Sandy moved quickly to commandeer a table toward the back of the room. Gaige walked over and put the cooler on the table.

"Keep that nasty thing off the tables as well," Jerry said.

Sandy looked at the cooler, "Those the samples?"

"They are." Gaige, still glaring at Jerry, moved so he could be certain to keep his eye on the counter that Jerry was theatrically scrubbing.

Sandy reached out to take the cooler, but Gaige pulled it back.

He said, "This place has changed. Used to be able to get a plain old cup of coffee here, or a Moxie."

Sandy tore her eyes away from the cooler. "Keeping up with the times. It's actually popular."

Gaige looked up at the menu board again and said, "I don't even know what that stuff is? Is it coffee?"

"I'm going to get something. Let me order something for you too." Sandy said.

Gaige shrugged.

Sandy settled a frothy cup of odd-smelling coffee in front of Gaige.

"So, here's the deal. Professor L'Heureux is getting Johnson out of town for a couple of days."

Gaige tilted his head and leaned in.

"Why is she going to do that? She hates Johnson."

Sandy leaned away from the table and laughed, "But Johnson doesn't hate her."

Sandy smiled and stirred her coffee.

"Turns out there's a Planet of the Apes Film Festival over in Conway, New Hampshire. L'Heureux asked Johnson to go with her. He jumped at the chance. They left this afternoon and won't be back until the day after tomorrow. That gives us a window of just over twenty-four hours in the lab. Plenty of time."

Gaige's mouth dropped open.

"Ewww. Why would L'Heureux do that?"

"You know that stuffy ancient literature class L'Heureux teaches?"

"Uh-huh."

"Well, you ever wondered how she can afford that car she drives on a professor's salary?"

Sandy leaned in.

"She's more than just a teacher. She writes true crime books under a pen name."

"True crime?"

Gaige thought about the string of high-end sports cars L'Heureux had driven when he was in school.

With a smug smile on her face Sandy said, "I've offered her an exclusive on the moose story."

Gaige scooted his chair from the table and folded his arms. Sandy took a sip from her coffee and waited on Gaige to respond.

Gaige looked at the samples and back at Sandy.

"I'm just not sure that —"

"Look. I know you have this thing about publicity. This gets us into the lab without having to fight with Johnson. I'm doing you a favor here. If it doesn't work for you, get another lab."

Gaige shuffled his feet.

Sandy was hoping Gaige would react this way. Now that the opportunity was presenting itself, she needed to move cautiously. She took another sip of coffee and wiped her mouth. Reaching across the table, she touched his arm.

"I know how hard notoriety is for you."

Sandy forced concern into her voice.

"I also understand that some sensational, tacky book is not something you want to be involved in. I'll just take whatever notes and other documentation, and work with L'Heureux. You don't have to be involved at all."

Gaige didn't want the media attention that would result from the book. He had been successfully hiding from the clam flat episode for several years. He looked down at the table.

"I'm worried that any true crime book is going to take away from what I'm trying to do. This moose needs to be cured."

Sandy nodded. She was brimming over with excitement.

"Okay. Tell you what. We need the lab. We have twenty-four hours with L'Heureux's help. I'll keep your name out of any publication regarding the work we do. How's that?"

Gaige regarded Sandy. He understood that this might be his one chance to get into a good lab. He began to tear little pieces off the edges of his napkin.

"Gaige, I'm handing this to you. Take the offer and cure the moose."

Sandy was right. He needed the lab to confirm his preliminary results.

"I'm up against the clock here and this is my one chance at a lab. Okay. Let's do this."

Chapter 35

Idalene hadn't gotten much sleep. She had spent the night adjusting her plan to salvage something from the wreckage of the press conference. The governor had stayed in the closet at the Grange until all the reporters had run off to chase after that odd woman who had bust in.

Her plan had to be altered. That was the unforgivable sin of last night's failure.

By the time Idalene arrived at the state house that morning, she was even more terrifying than normal. People, even those who didn't know her, scattered like prey as she approached, cowering against the walls as she walked by, or hiding behind closed doors.

To look at her, Idalene didn't appear to have gone without a full night's sleep. Every golden hair was in place, her makeup perfect, and her dark grey suit accentuating her long legs and highlighting her curves. When she walked, she floated. Her outward appearance was an active camouflage of what was going on internally. She had no time for people who might get in her way.

Heads would roll, there was no doubt.

Storming past Polly's desk, Idalene said, "Get that guy, Stanley or Sunderland, whatever his name is, over in Fish and Wildlife on the phone. I want to be talking with him as soon as I get to my desk."

Polly had most department heads on speed dial and was able to comply with Idalene's demand. Polly chirped into the intercom, "Stevens from Fish and Wildlife on line one."

"Stevens, I'm not sure we've been formally introduced. I'm Idalene Richie the governor's chief of staff. I was wondering if we had numbers on the moose population in the state?" she purred.

Stevens happened to be new to the state house and had not encountered Idalene before. If it hadn't been for the staffer he had to provide at the press conference, he would have had no idea who she was.

"I'm certain we do. I'll get those numbers to you."

Idalene's mauve fingernails tapped on the desk. "I'll wait."

Stevens' mouth set at the impertinence of Idalene. His voice sharpened as he said, "Let me put you on hold while I get those numbers."

"I'll be right here," Idalene said.

While she waited, she pulled up the bio on Stevens.

"You still there?" Stevens's voice came back on the phone.

"Yes. So how many moose do we have?"

"Around twenty-nine thousand at last count," he said.

Idalene stopped drumming her fingers on her desk.

"Are you quite sure that it's twenty-nine thousand? I heard that it was actually closer to fifty thousand."

Stevens snorted.

"Fifty thousand? No way do we have fifty thousand moose in this state," he said.

"Have they all been counted? What metric are you using to determine that number? Are you aware of the current crisis involving moose? Could it be that your department has underestimated the moose population and that is the underlying cause of these attacks? Gross mismanagement in your department has led to the deaths of people in this state. I hope you understand that we do have that many moose in Maine. They may be crossing the border with Canada. It may be that this Canadian migration is inflating the moose population. The herd needs to be thinned a little to avoid these terrible accidents."

Stevens was speechless.

Idalene waited.

"Stevens, did you hear me?"

"Yes, I heard you. Even if it were true that

Canadian moose were crossing the border, the moose population would be nowhere near fifty thousand."

"I want to be very clear about what you're basing your count on. Are you counting every single one?"

"Well, no. We —"

"So there is some discrepancy in the moose population count. You aren't certain about how many there actually are. I mean, after all, you don't account for each one. Seems there's a little wiggle room here."

"We base our numbers upon —"

"Of course you do. But does that take into account illegal foreign moose slipping across the Canadian border?"

"Foreign moose?" Steven's laughed. "What are you saying? That moose from Canada are actually targeting Maine? Are you serious?"

"Mr. Stevens, I am deadly serious. The people of this great state are at risk from moose overpopulation and you are making jokes."

Stevens raised his eyes to the ceiling.

"So you want me to say that we have fifty thousand moose so that you can thin the herd?"

"We do have fifty thousand moose. Some of them are from Canada."

Stevens was incredulous.

"You can't justify a kill-off. It's not even the season yet."

Idalene's voice was hard.

"Yes, I can. You need to show that we have fifty

thousand moose and need to thin the herd. Do I make myself clear? I see by looking at your bio that you're a smart guy. Your daughter's Facebook page says she needs braces and wants to go to [36]Hyde or Lincoln Academy for high school. Braces and private boarding schools are expensive." Idalene softened her tone. "I don't need an actual count, just something on paper from you that says we have fifty thousand moose. Got it? Good."

Stevens found himself without words again.

"I want your report on my desk in an hour."

Stevens listened to the dial tone humming in his ear.

He walked down to the deputy director's office and plopped down in a chair. "Otto, do you know anything about the governor's chief of staff?"

Otto blurted out, "Idalene!"

"I just talked with her and she wants me to lie about the moose population. Wants me to say it's fifty thousand," Stevens said.

"Then you had better say it's fifty thousand if you want to keep your job. If you don't, she'll destroy your career. I know I'll say whatever she wants me to. I have

36   Hyde School in Bath, Maine and Lincoln Academy in New Castle, Maine are high end boarding schools. One of Maine's big secrets is the number of Ivy League feeder colleges (Bowdoin, Bates, and Colby) found here and some pretty impressive high schools scattered around the state. Pretty good for a state with such a small population.

a family to feed."

Chapter 36

The West Bath selectmen and administrative staff had all been at last night's press conference and had recognized Harriet. None of them had wanted to let the press know who she was for very different reasons.

Frank and Mark felt they did not have permission to identify a citizen who had not committed a crime. Keith was afraid of her. Keith had run out a side door when Harriet had come in and was safely on his way home by the time the reporters left the grange hall.

The press conference had been a disaster. Instead of instilling calm, the governor had only increased panic. The phones had been ringing off the hook with calls from the press, neighboring municipalities, and campground owners.

"Town of West Bath, this is Mark."

"I'm over here in Georgetown. Look, I have campers here that are leaving. People are canceling reservations. They're afraid of your moose. What are you guys doing about it? How hard can it be to kill a moose? I'm losing business here," the campground owner said.

"I am sorry about that. We're working with the governor's office —"

"Big help that is. Didn't he run off the stage last night? You guys need to get a handle on this problem of yours before it destroys my business."

"Sir, I'm sure the law enforcement officials are doing everything they can," Mark said.

"I need to tell my campers something."

Mark rubbed his head. "Let me give you the number for Cumberland County. They'll be able to tell you more."

After he hung up the phone and walked into the Town Administrator's office.

"Frank, just got another call. This one from a campground in Georgetown."

"Let me guess, they want to know what we're doing about this problem," Frank said.

Mark nodded his head and shrugged.

"Tell people that the selectmen are holding a meeting tonight at the fire station. Better bring in more chairs. On second thought, maybe we should move the meeting to the school," he sighed.

"Give the superintendent a call and see if it's available." Frank had been standing at the window watching Lottie Day set up her protest in the town hall parking lot. Mark came over to stand beside him. Lottie already had a tent up and a small generator going. Her son, Larry was hammering signs into the lawn along the road.

"At least Keith stayed home today."

Mark nodded.

"Better get the Code Enforcement Officer in here to help Lottie with running power out there. How many extension cords do we have?" Frank asked.

Chapter 37

Gaige and Sandy, along with two underclassmen, had been working through the night. Gaige, fueled by cold Moxie and the two dozen whoopie pies he had purchased from a roadside stand, was tireless. Sandy, having received Gaige's verbal permission to leave him out of anything published about the work they were doing, fueled by her ambition. She had made a recording of their conversation at the coffee shop using her cell phone, just in case.

She had to admit, the research was fascinating. They had identified the organic ingredients contaminating the willow leaves and reached the conclusion that the venom from the black flies had been the activating agent. This project could indeed be used to make a name for herself.

The ultimate goal of finding a cure for the moose eluded them. For Sandy, it wasn't that much of an issue. She cared very little for the moose, other than using the poor creature for publicity. She also knew that once Johnson returned, she would still be allowed to continue her research in the lab without Gaige. She looked around, frowning at the encroaching piles of whoopie pie wrappers and empty soda cans.

"The sooner he's gone, the better," she thought.

Chapter 38

Gaige had been correct. The moose had crossed the New Meadows River in the predawn during low tide and made his way into Brunswick. Once again, he was driven by hunger.

The moose was chilled and wet as he headed west through the cold darkness, just ahead of the rising sun. Since the blackflies were no longer a deterrent, the moose was able to go steadily through the thick woods. When he reached the marsh, he caught the scent and stopped. There was a small swamp between the thicket and the big box store.

Here he would find food. He settled in to wait.

Benny Mudger's mother was scared to death to feed anything grown or made in Maine to her son. She was convinced she would accidently poison him because she had grown up hearing her father ranting about the dioxins and arsenic dumped into the water by the paper mills. She had studied these alarming pollutant numbers in high school health classes. When she got pregnant, she swore off anything that had the words "organic" or "made in Maine, or tap water." After she gave birth, she didn't feed her child anything that had been "made in Maine" or was labeled, "natural".

Benny had grown up eating fast food, prepackaged food, and no raw vegetables or fruit. Certainly nothing locally grown or raised. He drank soda.

As a result, he had always been roundish. His schoolmates referred to him as, "Benny the Pudger". Because of his eating habits, he also lacked any real ambition, preferring to work at fast food places because they gave him free food. Benny was currently working in a donut shop in the big box. He didn't like the early hours, but he did like the donuts.

As a result, Benny had never been contaminated with the dioxins and arsenic polluting Maine waters.

Benny's car chugged into the parking lot. The moose had noticed the coughing gray vehicle spewing visible clouds of noxious smelling fumes. The door to the vehicle squealed in protest and then finally opened. The moose watched leftover food bags fall out of the car along with other debris. He continued to wait.

Benny finally exited the car. His head bouncing in time with the music running from his cell phone through his earbuds. The moose rose as it watched Benny dancing to music the moose couldn't hear. Benny's strange behavior puzzled the moose and he decided to watch instead of approaching Benny. The moose settled back down in the tall grass keeping an eye on Benny as he disappeared behind the building.

The warming sun rose in the sky and people began to descend on the big box store. Several of the motorhomes parked in the store's lot were showing signs of life. The moose's interest grew as it watched the people arriving.

A small, but very distinct, inner voice pulled at the moose to flee. His ears twitched at the internal warnings. The busy nature of the area and constant movement of automobiles should have caused any moose to avoid the openness of the area. Another voice was stronger, more compelling.

Held in check by the smaller voice, the moose stayed hidden, watching and waiting. He lay down amidst the cattails, but did not sleep.

As the sun warmed its hide, the moose stirred.

"Hungry."

Hunger pushing back the small warning voice, the moose stepped out of the tree line into full sight of the shoppers. He moved slowly toward the parking lot, hesitating in the sandy area at the edge. While he waited, the shoppers saw him standing there.

"Look! There's a moose!"

People approached, taking pictures with their cell phones.

"Don't get too close. There have been reports of a moose killing people."

"It isn't attacking. It's just standing there. Look."

The shopper moved toward the moose. The moose watched and sampled the air.

The shopper moved within three feet of the moose. Dropping his head for a better smell, the moose snorted.

"Eww. The thing just blew snot all over me."

"Stay back. There's a moose that has rabies or

something running around," a tourist wearing an [37]Arkansas Razorback t-shirt said.

It was then that Benny left the store and headed for his car to take his morning break. The moose threw up his head as he caught Benny's scent again.

Benny had noticed the crowd and, not wanting to miss out on anything, joined them.

More shoppers, emboldened by the first adventurer, moved closer. The moose allowed them to approach as he carefully smelled the air. They formed in a semi-circle around him, positioning themselves to take more photos.

The moose waited. Over there, he could smell it.

"Different. Better. Hungry."

Benny took out his cell phone to snap photos.

Giggling, the couple from Arkansas moved to the front of the circle to get their pictures taken with the

---

37   **Razorbacks**: University of Arkansas symbol. A wild pig complete with tusks, going hell-bent-for-leather and wearing a scowl.

moose. The moose lowered his head again, extending his neck for a better whiff. There was a soft gasp from the crowd as they moved back a step or two.

The moose remained where he was and watched. After a moment or two, the crowd was emboldened to move back toward the moose. The moose twitched an ear and once again the crowd moved back.

The Arkansas man said, "Lands sake, people. This animal is nearly tame. Look here."

He boldly moved right up to the moose and placed his hand on the barrel-shaped body. The moose didn't even twitch. There was a collective giggle from the crowd.

The Arkansas man said, "Momma, come up here. Can someone get a photograph of us next to this animal?"

The moose's eyes scanned the laughing crowd.

They were caught unaware when the moose made his move.

Lurching at a speed no one was expecting, he knocked the Arkansas couple to the ground and stomped them to death before turning his dark eyes on Benny, who was still taking photographs. The moose charged, knocking Benny backwards, cracking his head on the pavement. The moose placed his huge gore-covered foot in the middle of Benny's chest, crushing his internal organs.

Benny lived long enough to see the moose chase down and kill two more people before the light faded from his eyes forever.

The phones lit up at the Brunswick police station as the panicked shoppers called in about the tragedy.

Chapter 39

With mounting anger, Idalene read the Washington Post story on the moose during breakfast. If that wasn't enough, she had received reports of yet another moose attack from the state police.

It was time to implement the West Bath selectmen's suggestion and deputize a posse of hunters to kill the thing.

There were already some vigilante groups forming so she had plenty of volunteers just waiting to be set loose. She pushed her car to speeds exceeding the limit and rocketed to the state house.

Once Polly's pain tolerance levels with her boss had finally been reached, the floodgates opened. Polly was a skilled administrative professional.

The icing on the cake was the fact that Idalene never paid much attention to Polly. Being undervalued by Idalene was working in Polly's favor.

The steady stream of information to her cousin,

New Hampshire's governor, was paying dividends. Today, Polly's observation of Idalene storming past her desk in a rage was the beginning of the big payoff.

***

"Oh, this is rich. The Washington Post picked up our story. 'Killer Moose Stalks Mainers.' And it comes from an unnamed highly-ranked source in the Maine governor's office. Excellent."

Governor Pickering smiled.

"Are we ready for the press conference?"

Governor Pickering stood and smoothed her suit. Checking her face in a mirror, she forced her grin into a concerned mask and made her way into the press room. Standing solemnly at the podium, she made eye contact with the members of the press in attendance, nodding at several from national news sources.

"Ladies and gentlemen, there's grave news coming from Maine. We are still trying to confirm the information, but our early investigations are causing us a great deal of concern. I'm certain you have seen the Washington Post today. We in New Hampshire are taking steps to protect our citizens against the incursion of what may be brain-eating moose coming across our border. I'm in contact with the National Guard. I want to let everyone across the country know that, in New Hampshire, we may not have ocean frontage like Maine, but we don't have killer zombie moose either. You are welcome here in New Hampshire, where it's just safer."

When the governor paused, the press corps erupted with questions.

Governor Pickering maintained her mask of concern and sorrowful look when asked if she had been in contact with the Maine governor.

"No. I'm sorry to say my colleague has not made contact with me, although I reached out to him this morning."

She stepped around the podium so there was nothing between her and the reporters.

"Speaking as a governor myself, I know Governor Pelletier must be focusing his full attention on dealing with this crisis. The State of New Hampshire stands ready to assist our neighbor. We will certainly accommodate anyone vacationing in Maine who wants to come to the safety of New Hampshire."

Chapter 40

The West Bath town office parking lot was home to a growing tent city, starting with Lottie erecting her tent smack dab in the middle.

Shortly after Frank arrived that morning, other people began to show up. Soon the parking lot was full of craft fair vendors who didn't appear to be protesting with Lottie.

A fried dough cart was setting up near the road.

Lottie appeared to be handing out information about combatting Satan, but most of the tents were sheltering folks hawking food and homemade crafts.

A particularly colorful tent with a large hand on the side was a temporary home to a psychic offering tarot readings. This psychic spent a considerable amount of time loitering just outside the town office's double doors, taking aura readings. She proclaimed loudly to the group at large that the aura for the town hall was, indeed, negative.

Keith had ridden his bicycle instead of driving his car so he wouldn't be recognized. Wearing a large hat and overcoat to disguise himself, he snuck through the back door. Walking upstairs, he found Frank staring out the window. He turned his attention to where his colleague was looking to see Lottie leap in front of an oncoming car.

"Save yourselves. The end is near! Take your children and loved ones and flee from Maine!" she cried.

Frank and Keith continued to watch as the car swerved to avoid Lottie before finding a parking spot on the grass on the other side of the road.

"Maybe we should have someone from the sheriff's department down here for crowd control. Someone's going to have an accident," Frank suggested.

"No police. We don't need the reporters finding out," Keith snapped.

He moved over to another window and slid the curtain back slightly. Peering out at the crowd filling the parking lot, he looked back at Frank.

"That crazy Day woman has them all worked up."

Frank looked at the growing number of people.

"Actually, the only one worked up is Lottie. The rest seem to be eating chowder and selling things," Frank said. "Looks more like an impromptu craft fair."

Keith gazed back out at the crowd.

"I think they've doubled in size in the last two minutes. Oh no! She just jumped in front of another car."

Keith rubbed his chin.

"She's going to get someone hurt or killed. That's all we need."

His body went rigid. Then he stepped back further from the window.

"I think I just saw a reporter. Is there any press out there yet that you know of?"

Frank scanned the crowd.

"Not that I can tell."

Keith muttered, "Could be bloggers."

Frank turned to Keith, "I'm sorry. I didn't hear you."

Keith glared at Frank. "If reporters do show up, say I'm unavailable. Tell them all the selectmen are unavailable."

Keith grabbed his disguise and headed down the stairs to the back door. He opened it a crack and when he was convinced the coast was clear, he jumped on his bicycle and hurried off.

Frank walked over to Mark's desk. "Go tell them they have to move some of those tents to the parking lot out back. They're blocking the entrance," Frank said.

Mark muttered under his breath as he left the safety of the building and walked toward the raucous crowd.

"Morning, Lottie," Mark said as he walked up to her.

"Oh, Mark, nice to see you,"

Lottie's eyes darted to the road.

"Excuse me a minute."

She ran back to the middle of the road and started shouting at another car. The driver pulled around her slowly and parked in an open spot at the edge of the pavement. Mark noted the long line of cars parked up and down the road.

Lottie returned.

"I've got to warn them. They're in danger!"

Mark nodded.

"The problem is the lot is filling up and these cars parked along the road may create a traffic--"

Lottie dashed out into the road again.

"—hazard."

He watched Lottie as she harangued the driver with dire warnings. Forced to stop, the driver noticed the craft fair and parked his car. Lottie rushed over to hand him a homemade pamphlet about the dangers of Satan.

Shaking his head, Mark turned to the row of small covered stands and approached the first table. The pleasant young man was busy packaging up a wedge of artisan cheese for a customer.

"We were wondering if you could move your tent to the lower parking lot."

The young dairyman said, "And I was wondering if you would be interested in this lovely cheese here. It's on special today."

About forty minutes later, Mark returned to the

town office with a bag of homemade donuts in one hand, and a half-eaten whoopie pie in the other.

Frank met him at the door. "Are they going to move?"

Mark finished swallowing a bite of whoopie pie and said, "Well, they really aren't blocking anything. They're going to tell new people to set up down there."

He wiped his mouth with the back of his hand.

"You should go get some chowder before it's gone. It's excellent."

Chapter 41

"We're almost there. I would ask that you stay on the ship until we get it tied up. I'll help you get your gear and trophies off after we dock. Did everybody have a good time?" the tour captain asked.

He surveyed the group, his eyes lingering on the young man from Omaha, who was still green around the gills.

"How are you doing there, Hank?"

"Oh, I reckon I'll be okay," Hank mumbled.

"For those of you who signed up for the celebratory dinner, I'll see you tonight."

Nudging one of the full coolers containing fish with his foot, he added, "We'll cap off the end of a successful deep-water fishing trip with our catches!"

Everyone but Hank cheered.

"For the rest of you, thank you for choosing Rising Sun Fishing Charters. I hope you'll come back and see us again. Be sure to tell your friends about us."

Zombie Moose

The fishing tour boat eased up alongside the dock. Gathering their equipment around them, the fishermen stood awaiting permission to debark.

Hank was just managing to stay on his feet. He stood nearest the edge of the vessel because he couldn't get off fast enough. He had been sick from the time he had set foot on the pitching vessel and had spent most of the excursion resting below deck. As soon as he could safely do so, he clambered over the gunwale and stumbled onto the dock. Falling onto his back, he felt the sway of the dock. Fighting his continuing nausea, he began to crawl his way toward the stability of the shore.

Through a seasick haze, Hank saw a dark shape blocking the end of the dock. He shook his head and refocused.

Pointing, he exclaimed, "Is that a moose? That's probably the ugliest thing I've ever seen."

He considered some of the fish that had been caught on the overnight trip.

"Well, one of the ugliest."

The attention of the group turned to the moose standing on the beach. The tour captain held up his hand and said, "Stay here folks, you don't typically see a moose out in the open like that. It could be sick."

Of course, members of the tour group pulled out their cell phones to snap pictures while the captain took a few steps toward the moose, who did not move, but sniffed the air and snorted.

The captain pulled out his phone and called his supervisor.

"I'm down here at Yeager's dock. We just got back. There's a moose just standing on the beach, blocking our way. He's not moving. I'm concerned because of those reports of problems with a moose."

"Man, you need to move away and get to safety. Is the tour group still there? You need to get them back on the boat now. That moose could be dangerous. There's been another attack this morning," the supervisor replied.

"I'm telling you, he's just standing here. I'm about ten feet from him and he doesn't appear to be aggressive. He's just standing here looking at us."

Just then, the moose made a sudden movement toward the captain, stopping just within a foot of him. He hurriedly backed away and exclaimed, "Saints preserve us."

He turned to the fishermen. "Get back into the boat!" The moose was only inches from him, yet the fishermen hesitated. He made a run for the charter boat as the moose snorted, blowing mucus all over his clothes before knocking him down. The captain's cell phone went flying from his hand, landing on the beach. The moose then turned on the stunned fishermen.

The fishermen scattered, some jumping into the safety of the boat while a few panicked and tried to make a break for the beach. Hank, faced with the prospect of an attacking moose or having to re-board the boat, rolled off the dock into the water. When he surfaced, he witnessed the moose stomping on his fellow fishermen who had attempted to escape across the beach, and eating their brains.

To the horror of the charter company supervisor, the captain, as well as the remaining live members of the tour group, could be heard screaming over the captain's phone. The moose stomped to the end of the dock, surveying the fishermen on the boat and Hank, who was clinging to the back of it.

The persistent hunger the moose had felt wasn't as strong. He eyed the water then turned away from the food floating in it. He sniffed as he walked past the weeping tour captain who had taken refuge behind a nearby rowboat.

By the time the police arrived, the moose had returned to the marsh and disappeared. The rescue crews spent over an hour attempting to convince the surviving fishermen that it was safe to return to the dock. Finally, an employee from Rising Sun Fishing Charters came out and piloted the terrified fishermen to the wharf in Bath.

Neither the fishermen nor the tour captain showed up for the scheduled celebratory fish fry later that evening.

Hank was on the next plane heading for the midwest.

Chapter 42

Idalene looked up from her computer and mashed a button on her phone. "Polly, have you found that blogger yet? We've got to stop him. That New Hampshire governor seems to have a direct line to whoever it is. Find him now."

Polly waited until Idalene's rant was over before returning to reading the paper. It had been a good day for her. Not only was Idalene's cover-up regarding the moose falling apart, but the position her boss had coveted with the senatorial candidate had fallen through, in light of the Washington Post article. Polly couldn't be more pleased.

It wasn't as if Polly had not technically tried to find out who was behind Sea Smoke. She had tracked the blog site to a Canadian host company, but had gotten no further. It appeared the writer did not want anyone to find out who he was.

Of course, Polly was only working hard enough

to make it look like she was making progress. Smiling, she continued reading the Kennebec Journal's article about the moose attacks that included mentions of Gaige's findings and some very clear photographs.

"This is excellent! She's going to go wild over this story."

Polly knocked on Idalene's door.

"What!" Idalene barked.

"I just thought you might like to see this article in the Kennebec Journal," Polly said.

She opened the door and walked in without permission.

"I don't want to see it," Idalene snarled.

"I need you to set up a press conference for the governor right away."

Polly gleefully noted that Idalene's hair was less than perfect. Not that it was messy, but some hairpins were coming undone and long curls were tumbling out of Idalene's signature French twist.

Also, Idalene's eyeliner was smudged. Overall she seemed a bit rumpled.

"Will the governor, or you, be attending the meeting in West Bath this evening?"

Idalene slapped both hands on her desk.

"Do you think I have time to sit in West Bath and hold the selectmen's hands?"

Polly continued to stand in front of Idalene instead of cowering like she normally did.

"The West Bath selectmen had our assurances in

writing that we would be in attendance, Ms. Richie."

Idalene made a fist and pounded the desk, sending papers flying, but Polly didn't react.

"Fine, you go. I'll expect a full report in the morning. Make certain you get that press conference set up."

"Yes, ma'am."

Polly walked back to her desk and emailed her cousin about the article before checking her inbox. Her eye's brightened as they scanned the messages. She opened a couple and grinned.

She had sent out a number of resumes yesterday and was surprised that some were responding so quickly. She took her time in forming a response to each of the requests for an interview.

One, in particular, held her interest for several minutes. She hadn't sent a resume to this employer, yet there was an interview request.

The investigators at the law firm Dean worked for had done a good job of tracing the source of the misinformation. Dean knew that it was coming from Idalene's office. He also knew that Polly had been expertly sabotaging Idalene by feeding information to the New Hampshire governor.

Polly had done a remarkable job of political maneuvering. Dean liked Polly's style and decided to reward her by having his firm strongly recommend her to the senatorial candidate.

While Polly had not known of her secret

benefactor, she was thrilled to be able to interview for the position Idalene had wanted so badly.

She glanced at Idalene's door. "Appears my resume is doing its job. Time to stop working for the Wicked Witch of the East," she mused.

Polly lacked any motivation to schedule the press conference and did the bare minimum necessary to make it happen.

Looking out the window she thought, "It's a beautiful day out there."

She walked down to the receptionist's desk.

"It's so nice out there, I believe I'll take an extended lunch break. After that, I'll be heading to West Bath for that evening meeting. I'll be back in the office [38]tomorrow afternoon sometime."

---

38   Polly's interview with the senatorial candidate was in the morning.

Chapter 43

The fire station was full to bursting when the meeting was called to order. Keith banged the gavel on the wood block.

"Come to order. Come to order."

The noise of the crowd reduced in decibels, but continued.

"Excuse me. We are having a meeting here and an agenda to get through. QUIET PLEASE!" Keith said as he banged the gavel repeatedly.

The crowd noise continued.

"If you don't quiet down so we can conduct town business, we will adjourn."

"Just like you, Keith, to run and hide your head in the sand. You never do face anything."

The crowd laughed and turned to the speaker.

Lottie Day stepped forward.

"Truth is, Keith, you don't know what to do. You don't have any idea what you're up against."

The reporter from the Times Record moved to a better position and started the recorder on her phone.

Lottie, warming to her story, turned to face the crowd.

"I saw the monster rise from the dead to kill and eat. It was in my own dooryard. It staggered out of the woods and collapsed. Not moving, not breathing, dead."

The crowd became very silent.

"Now, Lottie. No one is going to deny that you have had a traumatic experience. But let's not —" Keith said.

Raising an arm she pointed at Keith.

"Keith, say what you will. I saw it die, rise up, and kill that poor man. It was coming for me before I escaped. It's a zombie; a spawn of Satan. We need to arm ourselves. Get the little children out of here. Those of us that are able, that leaves you out, Keith need to organize and fight this evil."

Lottie turned, moving her pointing finger toward the audience. "We are paying for our sins. We need to turn from our evil ways."

"Ms. Day, you are out of order," Keith said.

"It's not a matter of order. It's a question of evil and you should quit trying to pretend it isn't. I came face to face with pure evil and was spared to warn you to flee from the devil."

"Excuse me. But I think the moose is suffering from a correctable chemical imbalance," Quinn stood and all eyes turned to her.

Lottie Day's mouth dropped open as she faced Quinn, her hand and finger still extended. The crowd returned to a low buzz. Keith turned to Quinn hopefully.

"Chemical imbalance? How so?"

"Well," Quinn looked around the room, "Reading the papers, it seems like someone is performing tests and has noted some anomalies. I think we should allow time for the scientists to examine those anomalies more carefully."

"Ah, yes, that seems reasonable. Are you personally aware of any work being done, or are you just reading the papers on this?" Keith asked.

"Mmm. Well, the reporters seemed to know about it."

Keith started turning purple. "The papers?" "Yes. It seems that the only choice here is that the moose is a demon when actually, it might just be sick," Quinn added.

"Young lady, we don't need to add more confusion to this situation." Keith grasped for a way to escape the ire of the crowd, "What we need are facts."

He pounded the table.

"Does anyone here have any facts?"

He glared around the room.

"No? Then maybe instead of becoming," he paused to glare at Lottie Day, "hysterical, we should let the authorities," he glared at Quinn, "handle this situation."

He looked around the room.

"We have a representative from the state present. We should let her comment."

Polly smiled and stood up.

Harriet had been sitting quietly when she remembered that she had left her wash in the machine and needed to put it in the dryer. As she rose, she thumped her cane on the ground and banged the chair in front of her with her bag.

The room went silent as every eye turned to watch her leave.

Lottie shouted, "The end is at hand! Repent!"

The crowd erupted and began to demand that the selectmen take immediate action.

Keith banged his gavel and shouted to be heard above the hubbub.

"Meeting adjourned. Officer, arrest anyone who doesn't leave. This is a disorderly crowd and constitutes to be a danger to the public good."

Keith glared at the uniformed man standing off to one side of the room. The officer bit his lip, placed his hand on his holster, and moved to the front of the room.

Besides the selectboard, Quinn was the only person in the room who remained seated.

The officer turned to Keith, "I'm not arresting Quinn."

"You can all come over to my house and we'll

figure out what to do," Lottie said and marched out of the room.

Keith whispered to Frank, "Put me in this situation again and you're fired."

The reporter was torn between finding out what Harriet knew, talking to Quinn, getting information from the representative from the state, or listening to what Lottie Day had to say. She looked at Quinn, sitting with her head bowed, then joined the crowd forming around Lottie.

Chapter 44

"No! Move that table over there. Get the flannel shirt off the governor and put that sweater on him," Idalene shouted.

"Will someone find Polly and fire her!"

Governor Pelletier sat at the back of the room, having makeup applied to his face. He was not in favor of holding this "fireside chat" but it was better than the press conference Idalene had planned at first. He never wanted to do another press conference. He was having nightmares about that woman where her eyes bore into him, laying bare the truth. Shivering, he focused on Idalene flitting around the room, bullying everyone. Tonight she seemed different, though, less in control. Still, she was attending to one detail after another.

Someone had placed a copy of his speech in his lap.

"I would never say anything like this. I can't say this on television," he thought.

Waving the makeup person away, he signaled for Idalene.

"Idalene, who wrote this? I can't say this. It's obvious that the moose is killing people. Even Governor Pickering knows there's a killer moose and is using this whole thing to scare tourists into leaving Maine."

Idalene ground her teeth and forced a smile.

"Governor, that hasn't been proven. Just a lot of speculation. We need to encourage people to use reason."

"I'm beginning to think that bad clams making heads explode is what is unreasonable. I also am beginning to believe that this LaRoche fellow isn't an environmental terrorist. I just can't say these lies. Everyone across the nation knows a moose is killing people here in Maine. Photographic evidence is all over the internet."

The governor flipped the speech onto the chair beside him.

"Can't we have Dave do this?"

Idalene cleared her throat and leaned in close.

"Governor, you have been worthless since the press conference the other night. Man up," she snarled. "If we keep saying this whole episode is about bad clams and ecoterrorism, people will believe it. We need to get on top of this before New Hampshire succeeds in drawing the tourists away from here."

Idalene picked up the speech and shoved it hard

against the governor's chest.

"You little coward. Listen to me and I'll get you through this. Just stick to what I've written and try to look like you have a backbone."

One of the cameramen said, "We're ready, Governor."

Idalene grabbed his arm and jerked him to his feet. The speech spilled onto the floor.

The surprised governor shot a threatening look at Idalene.

She smiled, but her voice was hard.

"Governor, remember FDR and his fireside chats? Well, this is your FDR moment."

Idalene all but pushed him over to his desk.

"Do what you're told and look concerned and caring. Your Teleprompters are over there. Just read the text," she hissed.

The governor, prompted by his fear of Idalene, adjusted the microphone and looked grim.

"I'm ready."

"Okay. In one, two, three. Rolling."

"My fellow Mainers, there has been confusing and contradictory information coming to you regarding unconfirmed reports of a killer moose. I understand your concerns. I, too, am concerned. We are working tirelessly to get to the root of these stories and find the truth."

"I want to talk for a few minutes with the people of Maine about this alleged moose issue. Authorities that have the expertise with these types of issues assure me that the moose is a shy creature who only becomes aggressive during mating season. Historically, there have been very few reports of a moose intentionally killing anyone."

"There has been a lot of speculation as to what may have actually occurred in West Bath. I want to urge the citizens of our great state to embrace reason during this time of uncertainty. Until we know all the facts, please refrain from making assumptions and engaging in unfounded speculation with regard to the events of the past few days."

"We do not know whether some people have died as a result of their own actions because of ingesting illegally harvested clams from closed flats, or if this unfortunate episode is an act of ecoterrorism. Sad to say, but it all could be just another underhanded and desperate ploy by neighboring states to draw tourists away from Maine."

"We have confirmed that moose from Canada have illegally crossed the border and have doubled the number of moose in our great state. This over-population may be the cause of some aggressive behavior in male moose. Just this afternoon, we have deputized skilled hunters to reduce this over-population problem, starting in West Bath. If there is, in fact, a killer moose, this culling of the herd will resolve that issue as well."

"We ask for your patience as we continue to

investigate these unsubstantiated claims that are circulating, much the same way that reports of Bigfoot and alien autopsies are. Mainers have always been levelheaded, hardworking, practical folks. Embrace reason and exercise patience until we can find the truth in this matter. Maine is and always will be the state where life is the way it should be."

Chapter 45

As Professor Johnson happily wooed Professor L'Heureux at the Planet of the Apes Film Festival, Gaige and Sandy worked non-stop, grabbing naps when they could. By sunrise, they were already awake and hard at it again. Sandy had sent one of the lower classmen out for more donuts, as well as more Moxie for Gaige. Time was running out, and they were no closer to finding a solution. Tempers flared.

"Gaige, will you clean up all these empty soda cans and whoopie pie wrappers? They're everywhere," Sandy barked.

Gaige continued to peer at the printout. "Gaige, are you going to pick that up or not?" Gaige continued to ignore Sandy.

"Fine. I'll do it," She reached across Gaige and snatched a Moxie can sitting in front of him.

"Hey, I'm still drinking that."

Gaige grabbed at the can, knocking it out of

Sandy's hand and into a plate containing what was left of a whoopie pie. The liquid sloshed over into one of the Petri dishes.

Gaige and Sandy looked at each other in stunned amazement, quickly turning to angry shouting.

"Oh, that's splendid. We only have a few samples left," Gaige yelled.

"If you weren't such a pig and disposed of your soda cans, we would still have that sample. This is exactly why you will never, ever, make it as a real scientist. You're a slob."

"Who you calling a slob? There was still plenty of soda in that can! You're the one that spilled it."

Sandy picked up a whoopie pie wrapper and threw it at Gaige. "You. I'm calling you a slob. We probably can't find a solution now because your samples are tainted."

"Are not."

"Are too."

While Sandy and Gaige argued, the underclassman noted that the Petri dish contaminated with the Moxie and the whoopie pie crumbs was bubbling. He took a sample and put it on a slide. After a few moments of adjusting the lens, he whistled softly.

"Hey, guys, you need to see this."

Unheeding, Gaige and Sandy continued to insult one another, shouting at the top of their lungs.

"Maybe you would feel better if you blew up Johnson's lab again. You seem to do that pretty well,"

Sandy screamed.

"That wasn't me," Gaige's eyes became large and he covered his mouth with his hand.

"Not you? Everyone knows it was you," Sandy said.

Gaige took a step back and began snatching up whoopie pie wrappers.

The underclassman raised his voice and said, "Excuse me. I think you need to look at this."

Gaige was the first to turn to the underclassman. "What?" Gaige asked.

The underclassman pointed to the microscope.

Sandy hovered over the instrument for several seconds, adjusting it twice. Standing up straight, she glanced up at the [39]clock before motioning excitedly for Gaige to take a look.

After looking into the microscope, Gaige glanced up at Sandy before checking out the slide again. He wondered why his knees felt so wobbly. He had to brace his hands on the countertop to steady himself.

---

39   History would record the time the cure was discovered to be 9:16 a.m., thanks to Sandy. This is her only real contribution to the discovery of the cure. Publically, however, she was the hero in this story.

Chapter 46

Professors Johnson and L'Heureux were having a late breakfast. Much to her surprise, L'Heureux was having a wonderful time. She found Yader Johnson to be funny, as well as a romantic.

It no longer bothered her that he wasn't as cool as most of the men she had dated. She enjoyed his company and had all but forgotten the reason she was there in the first place.

They had been reading the local weekly newspaper as they dawdled over their coffee, taking turns making up better stories to go with the headlines.

After an extraordinarily funny story, without thinking, L'Heureux reached over and held Johnson's hand. His bushy eyebrows rose, revealing sparkling brown eyes. Smiling, he patted her hand.

They stopped to get gas on the way back to the motel. L'Heureux ran into the convenience store for some sodas and snacks, leaving her phone on the passenger seat.

The annoying buzz of a text coming in caught Johnson's attention while he stood at the pump. Although he appreciated the convenience of cell phones, he felt that people tended to be addicted to them.

All the students always seemed to have their heads down, with thumbs flying. Seeing that L'Heureux had finally let go of hers pleased him. He glanced at the phone and saw the beginning of a text message.

"This is Sandy. EUREKA!"

He opened the door and picked up the phone. It was from one of his graduate students. He glanced back at the convenience store.

"Why is Sandy texting L'Heureux with a declaration of discovery?"

His curiosity overcame him and he read the rest of the text.

"This is Sandy. EUREKA! Cure found. LaRoche working on serum now. Safe to return to lab."

Having LaRoche in his lab was an immediate trigger for his temper. It took only a few seconds for his scientific mind to realize he had been played.

Johnson nearly crushed the phone in his hand. He turned and stormed toward the convenience store. Gesturing wildly, he confronted L'Heureux.

"You scarlet hussy! Did they pay you?"

L'Heureux was dumbfounded.

The cashier was entertained.

"Yader, what are you talking about?"

Speechless, he shoved the phone in her face.

Of course, as she read the text, she thought to turn the tables on him.

"You read my text?"

The cashier was now leaning on the counter, eavesdropping.

Johnson was no longer looking at L'Heureux. He had thrown cash in the general direction of the clerk to pay for the gas then stomped back to the car. He took his own cell phone from his pocket and called campus security, ordering them to remove LaRoche from the lab and have him arrested by the police for trespassing.

L'Heureux ran to catch up with him, but was too late. Johnson pulled away.

"Find your own way home, you shameless whore!" L'Heureux ran after him, but tripped on her handbag that Johnson had flung out the car window.

Numbly, she picked up the bag and wiped off the road grit.

"Guess I need to call a cab."

She looked at her phone again, rereading the text.

With a sharp glance in the direction Johnson was heading, she thought, "but first I need to warn Sandy."

Chapter 47

"Gaige. Gaige! Pay attention," Sandy said.

"I'm kind of busy here," Gaige snapped back.

"Well, you need to get busier. I just got off the phone with L'Heureux. Johnson knows what's going on and is on his way here. She thinks she heard him talking with campus security. You may only have a few minutes," she said.

Gaige turned to face Sandy.

"How did he find out?" Gaige demanded.

Sandy shifted blame. "I don't know. Maybe L'Heureux let something slip. The point is you need to get what you have and get out of here."

Gaige turned back to the lab station. "I think I have it, but this is a pretty crude serum," he frowned. "It should be tested."

"You don't have time. If security shows up, you'll have to leave anyway, and probably without the cure," she said. "Let me see the data."

Gaige began to bottle the small batch of serum he had just cooked up.

"I think you're good to go. If it doesn't kill the moose, I believe it will neutralize the toxin,"

Sandy said as she stepped back to let Gaige finish packing up what he needed.

"It's unfortunate, really. We're so very close."

Gaige placed the bottle in his backpack.

"I know. I know."

Sandy placed a hand on Gaige's arm.

"You're the one who Johnson has the problem with, not what you're actually doing. Why don't you leave all your notes here and I'll keep working on refining your serum? You can go find the moose and cure him with what you have," she said.

Gaige's eyes went to his notes and flashed back to regard Sandy.

"All right. You can bring--"

The door to the lab opened, causing Gaige to bolt to the far corner behind the back door.

The room was partially filled with students and Gaige's group had been working toward the back of the room. "I'm looking for," the guard looked at a notepad, "Gaige LaRoche," he barked.

"You," the security guard growled, pointing at a student, "Are you LaRoche?"

While the guard was distracted with the student, Sandy edged closer to Gaige's hiding place. She whispered, "There's an exit through the door down the hall. Go cure that moose!"

She then returned to the guard,

"Excuse me? Can I help you? I'm in charge here."

"I'm to escort Mr. LaRoche out of the building and deliver him to the police."

Moving closer, she said, "Who are you looking for again?"

The officer puffed his chest out and said, "I'm going to need to see some identification for each one of you. Line up over here."

After the guard had been satisfied that LaRoche was not in the lab and left to continue searching the rest of the building, Sandy recovered the notes Gaige had shoved into a notebook before his narrow escape. Smiling, she gathered them up and gave them to a student to make copies. As she was handing the pile off, she pulled a small map from the stack.

Looking at the triangulation sketched out on the map, she said, "So this is where he thinks that stupid moose is. If he does cure the thing, I believe I should be there as well. After all, I am leading this team."

Chapter 48

Idalene's blood pressure would not have made any doctor happy. The governor was hiding somewhere in the building, or at least she thought he was. According to the receptionist, Polly had decided to delay her arrival until this afternoon. The press was asking questions that were not going in the direction she wanted them to, either. In fact, a few just wanted to talk about what they were doing in New Hampshire to prevent any zombie moose from crossing the border.

She had to take action, but for the first time in years, she didn't know what action to take.

Picking up the phone, she called human resources.

"I want to place an ad for a new administrative assistant," she said.

"Oh, is Polly leaving?"

"No. I'm replacing her. She has abandoned her post," Idalene said.

"What?"

"She isn't coming in until this afternoon. She didn't ask me for permission. She's fired," Idalene said.

"Oh. Well, actually, she asked us for the morning off to take care of some personal business."

Idalene was speechless.

"She what?"

"She's taking some personal time, according to my notes here."

Idalene slammed down the phone and started chewing on her bottom lip. She thought her head was going to explode.

At this point, she was so spooled up, she jumped when the phone rang.

"What!" she commanded.

"Ms. Richie?"

"Yes! You're wasting my time. What do you need?" she shouted into the phone.

"Ms. Richie, some of the hunters think they know where the moose is."

Idalene could hear a distant roaring. She had something to focus on, something she could kill.

"Excellent. Where?"

She scribbled the location down.

"Tell them to wait for me. I'll be there in half an hour."

She started to press the intercom for Polly and remembered she was gone.

"You are so fired!" she screamed at the machine.

She grabbed her jacket and marched out the door. Stopping in front of the first secretary she saw, she said, "Get me a police escort. I'm going to West Bath."

Chapter 49

Quinn had grabbed the file her attorney had given her to review and stuffed it in her Bean bag. She planned on looking at the resumes today. She was not quite out the door when the phone rang. She wasn't going to answer until she saw who was calling.

"Gaige! Where have you been?"

"I got access to a lab. I think I have the cure."

"Oh, my goodness. Really?"

"I'm on my way to where I think the moose is to try to cure it before they kill it."

"Where? I'm coming!"

"That's a good idea. I think I may be in a bit of rouble."

Quinn rolled her eyes.

"I think that's just part of being you. Give me the location, and I'll make certain you have at least one friend when they arrest you for whatever you did this time."

Zombie Moose

After getting directions, Quinn realized the location was not in exactly the same place she had seen the moose the first time. Given the most recent attacks, though, the new site made sense. She ran upstairs to her computer to share the information with her blog followers, including nearly all the media outlets in the state.

Grabbing her camera and laptop, she ran to her car and headed to West Bath. Listening to the police scanner, she got Gaige on the phone.

"Looks like some hunters also have figured out the location. Gaige, buddy, you are in trouble."

Quinn arrived before anyone else and walked the short distance into the woods to wait for him.

***

Harriet McElroy was also closing in on the moose, but by accident.

Armed with her camera and binoculars, she was birding. She had spent a few minutes talking to the landowners and had gotten their permission to go into the woods behind their house. She had just reached a marshy clearing.

The moose, not fifty feet from where Harriet was walking, had noticed her, but she wasn't food.

Harriett had not seen or heard the moose. She was focused on a Eurasian Widgeon, perched in a willow tree at the edge of the clearing. Without making a sound, she crept up on the small bird.

***

Lottie Day was nowhere near the moose's location.

After the meeting at the fire station the night before, a large group of people had followed her home where they had formed the West Bath Smite Satan Society (WBSSS) and made plans to combat the evil that seemed to be manifesting itself throughout their town.

The next day, WBSSS commandeered a large parking lot near the intersection of Fosters Point and Witch Spring, since they realized the town office lot was just too small. Besides, this was a much more visible location.

Unfortunately, people looking for the moose were completely missing the newly set-up tent city. They either were turning before the lot to go down Fosters Point, or they were driving in via Congress Street from the east and heading down Berry's Mill.

***

When Frank and Keith arrived at the location posted on Quinn's blog, Sea Smoke, a large crowd of hunters, media, and on-lookers had already gathered. Keith was forced to shout, unheeded, from the back of the crowd.

***

Also standing in the growing crowd was Sandy. Unlike Keith, she wanted to remain unnoticed until she was certain the serum had cured the moose. Then with the documentation in her control, she would step forward and take credit for the discovery.

If the moose wasn't cured, she would get in her car and drive away to continue working on the cure without Gaige. It was a win/win situation for her.

***

Idalene arrived with the police escort following a mile or so behind her. The roaring in her head was getting louder and making it hard to see.

When she stepped out of her car, racial memory took control of the crowd. They instinctively parted to let her storm past them. The deputized hunter's racial memory also kicked in and answering an unvoiced order, they followed Idalene into the woods. The news crews loved the visual.

***

Gaige had arrived along with the first hunters. While the men confabbed about the best approach, Gaige slipped into the woods, unseen. Quinn had been watching for him and silently fell into step beside him as they made their way to the moose.

Chapter 50

Idalene set a quick pace. As she moved deeper into the woods, a guttural sound erupted from the back of her throat. She lost her Jimmy Choo shoes early on, sucked off her feet by the mud. She tossed her jacket into the brambles because it only slowed her down. With her skirt shredded around her legs and her silk blouse ripped and stained with blood, she ran through the woods, her golden hair flowing behind her.

The hunters became alarmed when they saw how Idalene was behaving. They fell back a few steps, letting her continue in her rampage toward the moose.

Gaige and Quinn had gotten to the moose first, however, and were crouching near the edge of the clearing behind a small group of hemlocks.

Quinn whispered, "How can you tell it's the right moose?"

"Well, I remember how it smelled. Just to be sure, though, I'm going to test a hair sample," he said holding up a small package. "It'll take a few seconds to confirm it."

"You can't walk up to that moose. It will kill you!"

"I don't think the moose kills native Mainers. Scott was just an aberration." Gaige stood up.

"It killed another Mainer yesterday in Brunswick," Quinn warned.

Gaige squatted back down beside Quinn.

"Isn't that interesting? I still think there's something about native Mainers that keeps the moose from killing them. I need some information on that latest victim," Gaige said.

Both Quinn and Gaige turned in the direction of the roaring from the woods.

"They're coming."

He looked towards the moose.

"No time like the present."

He stood and walked up to the moose.

The moose had been aware of Gaige and Quinn the entire time. He had smelled both of them before. They weren't food. When Gaige walked up to the moose and took a hair sample, he never flinched.

Gaige spent a few moments testing the hair. He turned to Quinn to give her a thumbs-up just as Idalene, in a full blood rage, erupted into the clearing.

Her hair was full of twigs and leaves and her face was streaked with blood. Mud had caked her legs and what was left of her skirt. She paused at the edge of the clearing, threw back her head, and howled.

Harriet had gotten some excellent photographs of the Eurasian Widgeon and was happily walking back into the clearing when she spotted Idalene making a ridiculous ruckus. Harriet hurriedly walked toward Idalene, thinking, she's going to scare off the birds.

The hunters appeared at the edge of the clearing, but none of them wanted Idalene to see them. She had gone totally berserk. She turned to the moose and emitted another howl.

"KILL IT!"

The hunters hesitated.

"But there's a man over there."

Idalene whipped her head around to the hunters.

"KILL HIM!"

Harriet bustled up to the hunters, asking the obvious.

"Are you hunters!"

Harriet was wicked intimidating without trying. When she scowled, everyone knew it could lead to their worst nightmare.

Terrified by Idalene, and also faced with Harriet and her judgmental melting stare-down, the hunters lowered their rifles and went back the way they came.

Harriet turned to Gaige, "Young man, what you are doing to that moose?"

"Ms. McElroy, the moose is sick. I think this serum will make it better."

Idalene turned on Harriet. A long buried ancestral Viking memory surfaced in Idalene as she considered Harriet. All the civilized barriers that had been erected by her family for centuries melted away as Idalene gave way to a berserker's blood rage.

A cultural memory buried deep in her psyche recognized the woman standing in front of her one of the peoples her ancient ancesters had encountered and conqureed as a [40]Scottish Pict. This one lone Pict was nothing in the face of Idalene's rage.

Idalene picked up a gun left by one of the hunters, aiming at Gaige, but because the gun was now full of mud, it missfired.

Idalene howled again.

Harriet's attention was now fully on Idalene.

Idalene planned on dealing with the worthless Pict after she killed the moose and anyone who tried to stop her. She grabbed the barrel of the gun and started swinging it like a club as she ran toward Gaige.

What Idalene didn't count on was Harriet's heritage.

True, Harriet was half Scottish, but she was also half Puritan with all the calm self-determination, sternness, and righteous indignation that goes along with it. Her two bloodlines met and shook hands at

---

40   **Scottish Picts**: Iron Age tribal people. The Vikings knew about them from their constant raiding of Scotland. Unfortunately, the Vikings didn't write much stuff down and we may not have known about them. However, the Romans just loved to write stuff down and recorded their encounters with the Scottish Picts.

that moment.

Harriet turned her cane upside down and finding a likely rock, she lofted it into the air like a golf ball, zinging it in a straight line right at Idalene. It hit her square on the forehead and knocked her unconscious. She fell with a slimy squish into the mud.

Calmly, Harriet turned to Gaige.

"Young man, I think you should take care of that sick moose now."

Gaige wasted no time and injected the moose, who commenced to shake and quiver before falling into a sound sleep.

Television crews ran into the clearing. They had witnessed the gibbering hunters running out of the woods and went in to get the story. They were there in time to see the moose being cured. Quinn had recorded the entire event with her video camera and quietly slipped back through the woods, unnoticed.

Chapter 51

Governor Pelletier's term in office was in shambles. Not only did his administration choose the wrong solution to the killer moose problem, but his chief of staff had been arrested attempting to kill the man who cured the moose. The governor had been listening to the news reports and commentary and had watched the video footage. Currently, he was weeping uncontrollably.

That woman with the accusatory glare was all over the news as well. They said her name was Harriet McElroy. He could not face that woman's soul-baring stare again. Her dark eyes cut through all the lies. She knew he was a fraud, and now some staffer he did not recognize had just told him he would be holding another conference.

What if that woman was there, watching him, calling him out on his lies? The governor's weeping turned to sobs and he began to tremble.

Looking at the other door to his office, he thought, "I'll just sneak out. What can they do if I'm gone? One of them will come up with a plausible story. I'll go to Canada or Vermont." He began to consider his options. "No. Some place warm with real beaches! Mexico! I'll hide in Mexico."

The governor dried his eyes and straightened his shoulders. Placing his hand on the door, he cracked it open and slammed it back shut.

"Reporters! How did they know about the back way out!"

He ran for the psychological safety of his desk. Cowering in his chair, his mind cast about for a way to escape. He looked at the window. "I could jump."

Placing his elbows on his desk and his head in his hands, he began to weep again. The intercom buzzed, filling him with dread. It was then that he saw the note on his desk calendar and suddenly felt some relief. He picked up the phone and punched in the number.

The governor's temporary chief of staff had been trying to alert him that there was only an hour before the press conference, but the governor was not answering the intercom.

The assistant had written the speech quickly and was proud of the way he had spun the entire event to look like Idalene was the villain. But where had the governor gotten to?

About a half hour before the press conference, the new chief of staff began to panic. With it being his first day on the job, and not even having actually been introduced to the governor, he was a little timid about just walking into his boss's office. Sweating bullets, he knocked on the door.

"No one's here right now," came a high-pitched voice from behind the closed door.

"Sir, is that you?"

Meanwhile, the governor looked around for a place to hide. The chief of staff could hear a chair scraping and soft thuds from inside the room.

"Sir, are you okay?"

No answer. He looked around for someone to tell him what to do, but there was only a secretary and she just shrugged.

"Sir, I'm coming in."

The door swung open and he took a step inside. There was no one in the room.

"Sir, are you here?"

A sotto voice from under the desk said, "The governor's not here. He's gone to lunch."

The puzzled aid moved across the room and bent over to look under the desk to find the governor folded up in the key hole covered with the state flag.

The sotto voice continued, "The governor is gone. Pay no attention to the man under the desk. Dave will be covering the press conference."

The aide stood up and tossed the speech he had written for the governor into the trash.

"Well, Dave won't need this speech."

Approximately twenty minutes later, Dave walked up to the podium and smiled at the reporters.

"Ladies and gentlemen, thank you for coming today. To re-contextualize the efforts to control impression management by a former staffer endeavoring to upsell themselves, misinformation implosions were created to misperceive the evidences. The corollaries emphasized by the actions of audacious academics at this self-same solar period pinpoint the disloyal performance of this discharged underling. The push back at the end of the day restored action items and best practices for a satisfactory postmortem for citizen end users. By trimming the fat, we are on the same page to future program outcomes."

Dave smiled at the group of reporters again.

"I will take a few questions now."

A reporter leaned over to his peer.

"Finally, someone who's talking sense."

Chapter 52

Quinn had gone back to her antique cape and uploaded the video to her blog. It went viral within half an hour, with national news sources reporting on it by the end of the day. She had noticed there was a message on her home answering machine on the way in, but had been in a hurry to get the video online.

The message was from Dean, her attorney. He wanted to know if she had taken a look at the resumes he had given her. Quinn had been putting off thinking about Dean's retirement, but now she reluctantly grabbed her Bean bag and reached for the file he had given her.

She noticed a bulkier, messy file crammed in the bottom of her bag, partially hidden under a couple of old newspapers. Wrestling the bulging folder from the depths of the bag, she saw the note scrawled across the front.

"Quinn, sorry about hiding this in your stuff.

Didn't want it to get lost. Gaige."

Since he was still at the police station, she took a look in the file, sensing that he wouldn't mind.

Spreading papers out on the coffee table, she went through the file's contents. Similar to the research Gaige had conducted on the cure for the moose to date, it appeared he had been secretly taking that research in an entirely different direction.

After a few moments she smiled and said aloud, "Gaige, you devious little devil."

Epilogue

The moose became a huge tourist draw for West Bath. After a brief dispute between PETA and the University of Maine, the moose was tagged and released back into the general West Bath area. He developed quite a taste for Moxie and whoopie pies.

He could be found during the summer months loitering around State Road and Fosters Point Road. He moved between Walter's whoopie pie stand and the New Meadows Market caging snacks from everyone.

***

Walter continued to sell whoopie pies and made friends with the moose. Tourists were safely able to get pictures taken with the moose and Walter for a small fee.

***

Lottie abandoned her whoopie pie enterprise and began writing books on combating Satan. She was often seen hiding in the woods and annoying the neighbors around Walter's whoopie pie stand. She

wanted to be there to combat Satan in case he returned.
***

Idalene finally became an international name. The videos of her running into the woods in berserker mode went viral. She now works as a toll collector at the Maine/New Hampshire border. She's the one with the perfect manicure.
***

Polly got hired by the senatorial candidate who won his election by a landslide with her help.

Polly is now in Washington D.C. and has her own staff. When she returns to Maine, she flies into Manchester or Boston just so she can drive through Idalene's toll booth.
***

Benny "the Pudger" Mudger gained fame post mortem as being the only other native Mainer killed by the moose. Sandy had determined that Scott was the first kill only because the moose didn't yet know it disliked the taste of dioxins or arsenic. Benny had never had any native or organic foods so was never contaminated with those pollutants. News about Benny created quite the upsurge in eating locally grown foods.
***

Quinn's video of Harriet using her cane to send a rock at Idalene also went viral. Because of the perfect golf swing she used to send the rock flying, Harriet became the darling of golf clinics everywhere. In addition, her photographs of the Widgeon won international awards.

***

Governor Pelletier resigned citing health reasons and moved to Mexico. Dave was called in to handle the transitioning process until a new governor could be elected. Dave was urged to run by both parties, but declined because he made more money being a meeting substitute.

***

Egan Tyler's cowardly ways caused him never to rise any higher than lab technician. He finally took a job at a pet food company because they paid so well and his harpy of a wife was complaining about having no money.

***

Zoe L'Heureux and Yader Johnson's long-standing roles had reversed. L'Heureux now pined after Johnson who was at best indifferent. This may have been the reason that L'Heureux shifted from writing true crime books to crafting torrid romance novels.

***

Professor Johnson dreaded this trip. He disliked fundraising. He had reluctantly agreed to go because it wasn't like they were actually begging money from this insect repellant company. The owner had offered it.

It didn't make him feel any better that the college president, Nicholas Fulman, was with him. Standing on the sidewalk looking up at the shiny corporate building only irritated him.

"Oh, come now Yader, you're going to get a new science building out of this. You can be nice for half an hour," Nicholas said.

Johnson frowned at the pavement and thought, A science building named after this repugnant merchant. "Let's get this done then," he said.

They passed through the foyer, stopping at the reception desk for guest badges and to get directions. Johnson was unimpressed. He glared at the corporate name emblazoned on the wall as they passed by it on the way to the elevators.

"A few years ago this guy was nothing. Nothing. It was dumb luck that he developed this bug spray."

The college had made quite a name for itself because of Sandy's role in curing the moose, but they had never been able to duplicate the zombie effect. It was just all academic study and research; nothing marketable.

The bug spray had taken the world by storm. It was environmentally safe, made from all renewable organic materials, was not toxic to anything except insects, and, Johnson had to admit, didn't smell bad or sting your eyes.

The inventor had made a vast fortune on his patented formula and crushed his competitors.

The elevator reached the appropriate floor, the door sighed open, and the two of them stepped out onto the soft carpet. The receptionist stood to greet them.

"President Fulman, Professor Johnson, can I interest you in something to drink while you wait? Mr. LaRoche will be with you shortly."

Sadly, Marsha's life path was hindered by being born a Chicago Cubs fan and often thinking things are funny that no one else finds the least bit amusing. Other than these disappointing genetic traits, she enjoys living in Maine with her wicked smart husband and wicked smart daughter.

Coming Soon

Jeezley Pirates
of West Bath, Maine

Coming Soon!

Want more quirky Maine residents behaving oddly? Jeezley Pirates is your next read! This stand-alone novel contains prehistoric pigs, violent French-fry eating sea gulls, faked artifacts, diabolical real estate agents, rabid treasure hunters, and, of course, Jeezley Pirates. Loosely based on the maybe true story of the Dread Pirate Dixie Bull.

SOUVENIRS

By Marsha Hinton

"You're a hero," they said.
"You saved lives that day,"
they said.
Kara didn't feel like a hero.
She felt like damaged goods.

* 9 7 8 0 9 8 8 2 0 3 6 2 4 *